Candy Canes and Cadavers

Sapphire Beach Cozy Mystery Series
(Book 4)

Angela K. Ryan

John Paul Publishing

TEWKSBURY, MASSACHUSETTS

Angela K. Ryan
John Paul Publishing
Post Office Box 283
Tewksbury, MA 01876

Publisher's Note: This is a work of fiction. Names, characters, places, and incidents are a product of the author's imagination. Locales and public names are sometimes used for atmospheric purposes. Any resemblance to actual people, living or dead, or to businesses, companies, events, institutions, or locales is completely coincidental.

Cover Design © 2019 MariahSinclair.com
Book Layout © 2017 BookDesignTemplates.com

Candy Canes and Cadavers/ Angela K. Ryan. -- 1st ed.
ISBN: 978-1-7340876-2-8

A Note of Thanks from the Author

I would like to warmly thank all those who generously shared their time and knowledge in the research of this book, especially:

Jacki Strategos, Premier Sotheby's
International Realty, Marco Island

Carol Buccieri
Bella Stella Beads, Haverhill, Massachusetts

Marco Island Fire Rescue
Marco Island, Florida

Any errors are my own.

Chapter 1

DURA'S WARM VOICE FLOATED through the phone and tugged at Connie Petretta's heartstrings. Although Connie's dear, longtime friend was eight thousand miles away in Kenya, modern technology made it feel as if they were sitting across from one another.

Excitement spilled from Dura's words. "I'm so happy that our plan is coming to fruition."

Connie could picture her friend's eyes dancing with joy the way they always did when she was helping others.

Over email, Connie and Dura had hatched a plan for a special fundraiser whose proceeds would go toward a project at Dura's church, a church that Connie also attended during her two-year term of volunteer service after college. The parish had a nutrition center that drew hungry families when their situation became desperate, but, since the parish was poor too, the church had little or nothing to offer lately.

During one of their online conversations, Dura was lamenting over their predicament, and the two women came up with an idea for a project they had affectionately dubbed Operation Chicken Coop. They would raise money to build and fill a chicken coop so the parish would have eggs to provide lifesaving food for local families. Any extras could be sold at the local market to cover other needs. The eggs would provide local families with much-needed protein and Vitamin A, both of which helped prevent blindness, as well as other issues connected with malnutrition, in children.

"Did you receive the estimate I emailed to you?" Dura asked.

"I'm looking at it right now." Connie glanced through a printout of the estimate, which itemized the cost of building materials, chickens, vaccinations, and food. The labor would be donated by residents of the village. If they could raise four thousand dollars, they would be able to build a large coop and purchase enough chickens to benefit many families in Dura's village.

"Do you think you'll be able to complete all the earrings we'll need and sell them before Christmas?" Dura asked.

Connie ran a hand through her dark, shoulder-length hair. "It's a tight timeline, but with some hard work and a lot of prayers, I think we can pull it off. If we sell each pair for twenty dollars we need to make and sell two hundred pairs of earrings in the two weeks between now and Christmas to meet our goal."

Fortunately, Connie's Thursday evening jewelry-making class had committed wholeheartedly to spending the next two Thursday evenings, and as much time as they could spare at home, to creating the candy cane earrings, and Connie had already made fifteen pairs since the supplies arrived yesterday. With Christmas right around the corner, business was strong at *Just Jewelry*, which was Connie's store where she sold her handmade creations, as well as Fair Trade pieces from Kenya and Ecuador. "We'll get it done," Connie said, trying to convince herself as much as Dura.

Connie was thrilled to be working with Dura on this project. The two had been close friends since Connie's postgraduate term of volunteer service. In fact, it was Dura who taught Connie how to make jewelry, instilling in her a lifelong passion for the craft. So much so that, last year, after inheriting a beachfront condo from her aunt and namesake Concetta Belmonte, Connie relocated to southwest Florida to open a jewelry shop, combining her love for jewelry making with her passion for humanitarian work. Dura was one of her Fair Trade artisans and her biggest supplier.

As soon as Connie hung up with Dura, she resumed pacing the weathered hardwood floors of *Just Jewelry*, stopping at the front window every few seconds to check for her family, due to arrive from the airport at any minute. Between the fundraiser and her family's visit for Christmas, it would be a hectic couple of weeks. Connie couldn't wait for them to see *Just Jewelry*. The grand opening had been in April, but this would be the first time her parents, sister, brother-in-law, and twin three-year-old niece and nephew would see the store. She didn't know what she was more excited about: her family's arrival, it being her favorite time of year, or the nutrition center project coming to fruition. Connie felt like a child on Christmas morning, and Christmas morning was still two weeks away.

"Staring out the window is not going to bring them here any earlier," Grace Jenkins, Connie's friend, neighbor, and employee said. Grace had agreed to work that evening instead of her usual morning shift, so Connie could return with her family to Palm Paradise, the condominium building where she lived, and help get them settled.

Connie sighed. "I know. I should be making candy cane earrings instead. But I can't sit still."

Ginger, the Cavalier King Charles Spaniel that Connie had also inherited from her aunt, looked up every so often from the plush rug under the glass coffee table in the store's seating area. Connie and Grace had been scurrying around all afternoon, making sure that everything was looking its best, and sweet Ginger seemed to be wondering what all the fuss was about.

Shortly after 6:00, two mid-sized cars pulled up in front of her store. Connie squinted as she peered into the passenger side window of one of the cars. She'd recognize her mother's long, dark hair anywhere. Her family had arrived!

Connie's parents, Josephine and Greg, exited their car first. Connie smiled as her mother pointed excitedly toward the storefront, with a gentle breeze from the nearby Gulf of Mexico pushing back her hair. Connie's father hopped out of the driver's seat wearing a broad smile. The next to emerge from their rented cars were Connie's sister, Gianna Bianchi, and brother-in-law, Gary. Their three-year-old twins, Noah and Hannah, waited to be freed from their car seats.

Connie's heart raced with excitement. Until she saw their faces, she hadn't realized how much she missed them.

Jo and Greg were the first in the store. Jo squealed as she ran over to Connie, who was already halfway to the door. The two women embraced until Greg eventually broke them apart so he could hug his daughter, as well. Shortly behind Jo and Greg were Gianna and her family. It was only a three-and-a-half hour flight from Logan Airport to the Southwest Florida International Airport, but with a couple of energetic three-year-olds in tow, Connie wasn't surprised that Gi and Gary looked like they had just run a marathon.

Connie bent down to embrace the twins as they ran into her arms.

"How did these two do on the flight?" Connie asked.

Judging from the weary expressions on their parents' faces, Connie already knew the answer to that question.

Gianna shrugged. "Could have been worse, I guess."

Connie hugged her weary sister and brother-in-law, then gave her family the grand tour of *Just Jewelry*. She began with the Fair Trade section, which she was most proud of. It contained an array of handmade jewelry from Kenya and Ecuador, some in muted earth tones and others in vibrant blues, greens, and oranges. Then they moved on to the rest of the store, including the circular checkout area in the middle and the storeroom out back. Next, she brought them to the large oak table where she and her students created their jewelry masterpieces.

"This dentistry cabinet is such an exquisite piece," Jo said, referring to Connie's creative storage solution for her beads and other jewelry-making supplies.

Next, they took a moment to admire some of Connie's handmade pieces on the displays beneath the driftwood accent wall. Connie ended the tour in the seating area by the Fair Trade section, where two delicate armchairs face a red loveseat.

Connie and Grace brought out some iced tea, which Connie had brewed extra strong, anticipating her family's travelling fatigue, and joined the others. They also pulled over two extra chairs from the table. Grace had been a friend of the family for more than ten years, so everyone was ecstatic to see her, as well.

"I almost forgot how beautiful your jewelry is," Jo said. "I'm glad you are sharing your talent with the world."

"I don't know about the *world*, Mom," Connie said. "But at least the residents and tourists who visit Sapphire Beach."

Gianna scanned the store as she sipped her tea. "I have to say, sis, that Mom's and my decorating experience has rubbed off on you." Jo and Gianna owned a home staging company back in Boston and were the professional decorators in the family.

Connie smiled proudly. "I learned from the best."

When everyone finished their drinks, Connie offered to bring them back to Palm Paradise to settle in. Gianna, Gary, and the twins were staying at Connie's, while Jo and Greg would sleep in Grace's spare bedroom. Four houseguests would make it tight at Connie's place, but she insisted. She wanted to spend as much time with her family as possible, and she was afraid if they stayed in a hotel, she wouldn't see them as much.

"You know where I keep the spare key," Grace said to Connie. Then, to Jo and Greg, she said, "Just make yourselves at home. The refrigerator is full, and there is a bottle of wine on the counter."

"Thank you," Jo said, embracing Grace. "We are so looking forward to spending time with you during this visit. It's been too long."

In three separate cars, Connie and her family made the one-mile commute along Sapphire Beach

Boulevard to Palm Paradise and lugged the suitcases upstairs.

"I forgot how much stuff these little guys require," Connie said, throwing a couple of duffel bags over her shoulders.

While the others unpacked, Connie took the pan of baked ziti she had prepared that morning out of the fridge, put it in the oven, and made a salad. Within forty-five minutes, everyone gathered around the dining room table.

They said the blessing together and dug into their dinner.

"So, the play is Friday night?" Greg asked, directing his question to nobody in particular.

The family had come a full two weeks before Christmas so that they could attend a production of "A Christmas Carol" at the Sapphire Beach Playhouse. Being a former actress, Concetta had served as the Chair of the Board of Directors for the theatre, and the play was being performed in her memory. Damian Pritchard, the executive director of the playhouse, had reached out to the family and personally invited them to opening night.

Connie nodded. "The play opens on Friday night, but we've also been invited to a Christmas party at Damian's home tomorrow night." His parties were legendary. Damian, who would play the role of Scrooge this season, owned a beautiful Gulf-front mansion. Concetta often came home to Boston for Christmas but would always make it a point to remain in Sapphire Beach until after Damian's party. Anything that Concetta enjoyed that much had to be special.

Greg and Gary exchanged a glance.

"Sounds like fun," Greg said. "But Gary and I have decided we'd rather stay home and watch the twins while you ladies and Grace go to the party. It's not really our thing. We'll do something fun with the kids instead."

"That's not a bad idea," Gianna said. "It will save us from having to find a sitter on short notice."

"In that case," Connie said, "let's not waste their invitations. I'll invite Elyse and Stephanie." Elyse had been Connie's realtor, and the two had become fast friends when Connie relocated, and Stephanie, also a good friend, was Grace's daughter.

"Why not invite your cop boyfriend instead?" Jo asked.

Detective Zachary Hughes wasn't exactly Connie's boyfriend. They went on a first date last March, and, due to a miscommunication and both of their unusually busy schedules the past few months, they hadn't yet made it to their second date.

"Mom, I promise to introduce you to Zach before you leave, but please remember that we've only been on one date."

After a long day, everyone decided to call it an early night. Connie and her parents cleaned up so Gianna and Gary could put the twins to bed. Then, they all retired for the evening. Connie took advantage of her free time to make some candy cane earrings with materials she had brought home. She was bound and determined to make this fundraiser a success.

Chapter 2

CONNIE WAS AWAKENED EARLY Thursday morning to the sound of musical laughter floating through her bedroom and four tiny hands shaking her shoulders. Hannah and Noah were kneeling over her on her bed.

"Guys, it's not even 6:00 AM." She had been planning to wake up a little early to play with the twins before heading into the shop, but not quite *this* early. However, since they clearly were not going to permit her to sleep any longer, she tackled them onto the bed and tickled them until their giggling turned into a roaring pitch. Their precious laughter melted both her heart and her fatigue.

Connie put some waffles in the toaster for the twins and made herself a protein smoothie and a strong cup of coffee. After breakfast, Connie and the twins played in the living room until Gianna and Gary woke up, and her parents made their way over from Grace's.

Ginger followed her to the door as she left for work, so Connie bent down and scratched the dog's head. "You'll get more attention if I leave you home today, sweet girl."

Before leaving, she glanced back at her sister, Gary, and the twins, who were chatting away as Jo and Greg sipped their morning coffee. She did enjoy her peace and quiet, but she had to admit, her condo felt more like a home with everyone there.

Connie arrived at *Just Jewelry* without a minute to spare and was thrilled to see Grace's note that she had sold seven pairs of candy cane earrings the night before. Grace had undoubtedly been talking them up, but they still had a long way to go to meet their goal. Connie didn't waste any time getting to work.

At the oak table, she set up the tools and materials she would need to make more earrings. She began each earring by cutting a piece of 22 gauge wire, straightening it, then making a loop at the bottom with her round nosed pliers. Next, she strung the red, green, and clear Swarovski crystal beads until she had added all but three. Then she strung the silver-plated ear wire loop, the piece that attaches the earring to the ear, and added the remaining three beads. Finally, after making another loop at the top, she bent the earring into a candy cane shape. When both earrings were complete, she attached them to an earring card and set aside the newly completed pair. With a little practice under her belt, she was getting fast. Each pair took less than ten minutes to make.

After lunch, Connie posted some pictures of the earrings and information about the fundraiser on her website and social media accounts to help spread the word. When she finished, she closed her laptop and gazed out the front window, trying to think of creative ways to advertise.

It turned out the answer was right in front of her. Literally. She could use her display window to promote the earrings.

Connie stepped outside to study the Christmas display that she and Grace had created after Thanksgiving. A small, artificial tree, which sat on a blanket of faux cotton snow, was decorated with an assortment of necklaces and bracelets that hung from its branches like ornaments, and wrapped jewelry-sized boxes sat beneath the tree as if awaiting Christmas morning.

The rest of the window contained various jewelry displays, featuring an assortment of her best red and green pieces scattered throughout. Right in the center of the display was the perfect spot to add the candy cane earrings.

Within her boxes of Christmas decorations out back, Connie found a miniature red Christmas stocking and laid it on the cotton snow with earrings spilling out. Each pair was attached to a black velour earring card, which provided the perfect backdrop for the red, green, and clear crystal beads. Then she added a printed description of the chicken coop project to an antiqued gold frame and placed it next to the stocking. She stepped back to admire her handiwork, pleased with the finished product.

Then Connie set aside twenty-five pairs for a special order that Damian had placed and put the rest of what she had made so far in a small basket by the checkout register, along with another framed description of the project. She hoped people would not only buy them for themselves, but also as Christmas gifts for friends and family.

The rest of the day flew by, and, before Connie new it, Abby had arrived for her evening shift. Abby Burns, Connie's only other employee, had agreed to cover the store that evening so both Connie and Grace could attend Damian's Christmas party. Connie's jewelry-making class was scheduled to meet at 7:00, but since the plan was to make candy cane earrings, Abby could handle leading it. Abby, a senior English major at nearby Florida Sands University, had been part of Connie's first jewelry-making class back in June and now worked evenings and weekends at *Just Jewelry*. Although she was young, Abby was responsible and mature, probably as a result of some serious health challenges she had faced during her teenage years.

True to her industrious spirit, Abby came through with a dozen pairs of candy cane earrings she had made at home the previous night. Since the Christmas party didn't start until 7:00, they spent the next hour making earrings and chatting. Connie had come to love reliving her college years through Abby.

"Promise me you'll take plenty of pictures at the party," Abby said.

"It will be like you were there with us," Connie said.

When it was time to leave, Connie took the box of earrings she had set aside, hopped in her silver Jetta, and drove home to get ready for the party. She had texted Elyse and Stephanie last night, and they were thrilled about coming to both the party and to the opening performance of "A Christmas Carol" the following night.

As Connie turned into Palm Paradise, the sun was setting over the Gulf of Mexico, leaving in its wake a soft orange sky hovering above the sapphire waters. The tall coconut palms that flanked the expansive driveway, leading to the white condominium building that Connie called home, were wrapped in white holiday lights.

Connie punched in the security code and pulled into the underground garage. Upon climbing the staircase that led to the lobby, she was greeted by a substantial tree decorated with blue and silver ornaments. The anticipation of a festive evening ahead with her mother, sister, and dear friends suddenly filled Connie with excitement.

She accessorized her favorite black dress with a red multi-strand coral necklace and a matching bracelet and earrings. Between adding the candy cane earrings to her display window, all the holiday decorations, and dressing for the party, Connie was officially in the Christmas spirit.

Connie, Jo, and Gianna went downstairs to wait for the others in the lobby.

"I cannot wait for you both to meet Elyse and Stephanie," Connie said. Although Stephanie was Grace's daughter, she had only recently moved to town, so she hadn't yet met Connie's family. And Connie had only met Elyse when she put Concetta's condo on the market last January. Elyse's persistence and friendship played a large role in Connie's decision to relocate to Sapphire Beach from the Boston area.

"I feel like we know them already," Jo said.

Grace exited the elevator, looking elegant in a cranberry silk dress that complimented her medium-length gray hair.

"You look amazing, Grace," Gianna said.

"Do I?" she said, nervously checking herself in a nearby mirror. "Thank you, honey. I used to go to so many fancy parties with Concetta, but it's been a while."

When Elyse and Stephanie arrived, Jo and Gianna hugged them as if they were old friends. Elyse and her husband, Detective Joshua Miller, were in the process of adopting a three-year-old child named Victoria, who currently lived with them as a foster child, so it didn't take long for Gianna and Elyse to make plans for a play date as soon as Elyse had a free afternoon.

Since there were six of them, they took two cars, and within ten minutes, they were parked in front of one of the most exquisite mansions that Connie had ever seen.

"Wow," Jo said, taking in the majestic structure before them. "I almost forgot how wealthy some of my sister's friends are."

The home's rich, cream-colored stucco and flower-pot roof gave it a warm, Mediterranean vibe, and the brick pavers beckoned guests to the front door. Palm trees of various sizes and varieties punctuated the front yard.

"This home is easily worth three million dollars," Elyse said.

"I'll bet you could live for a year on what this house would bring in commission," Stephanie said.

"Well, let's stop gawking. We have a party to attend," Jo said.

Connie retrieved the small box of candy cane earrings from the trunk of her car.

"What's in there?" Elyse asked.

Connie opened the box revealing the earrings to the women.

"Those are so cute," Elyse said. "Did you make them as a gift?"

"Not exactly." Connie explained about the fundraiser and Operation Chicken Coop. "When Damian stopped by *Just Jewelry* to invite us to tonight's Christmas party, I was in the process of working out the details with Dura, so I happened to tell him about the project. He thought it was such a good idea that he ordered twenty-five pairs of earrings for the cast and asked me to bring them tonight so he could hand them out at the party."

As the women made their way down the long driveway, Connie asked Grace, "How exactly did Concetta know Damian?"

Grace smiled as if reliving a happy memory. "Damian and Concetta went way back. He was a successful actor who, like your aunt, retired to Sapphire Beach, although for different reasons. While Concetta was looking to live a quiet life away from the Hollywood scene, Damian relocated to accept a position as executive director of the Sapphire Beach Playhouse."

"Weren't he and Auntie Concetta in a movie together when they were young?" Gianna asked.

"Yes, that's how they originally met," Grace said. "When Damian heard that Concetta was living here, he convinced her to be on the Board of Directors. She loved the connection to the arts and eventually was elected as Chair of the Board. Since Damian knew how much Concetta loved 'A Christmas Carol,' he proposed that the company perform it this year and dedicate it to her memory."

Just as Connie was about to ring the doorbell, she noticed a tear glistening in Gianna's eyes.

"Are you okay?" Connie asked.

"It's just so strange to be in Sapphire Beach without Auntie Concetta."

Judging by the look on her mother's face, she shared her youngest daughter's sentiment.

Connie looped her arm through her mother's and sister's arms. "I know. It was hard for me to be here at first, too. And it still is sometimes, because memories of her are everywhere I turn. But it brings me comfort at the same time."

Jo nodded and forced a smile. "We'll get there, too. One thing I know for sure is that Concetta would be thrilled that we are all here tonight."

Grace rang the doorbell, and they were greeted by a woman with short blond hair and blue eyes, who appeared to be in her early sixties and to have come straight from a spa.

"It's lovely to see you again, Grace," the woman said, giving her an air kiss. "This must be Concetta's family and friends."

Grace introduced the others.

"I'm Sophie Michel-Pritchard, Damian's wife. It's so lovely of you to come," she said, ushering them into the house and toward a distinguished-looking

23

man with dark eyes and gray hair. "Damian, darling, Concetta's group is here."

Damian excused himself from a couple he was talking with and joined the women. "How lovely to see you all," he said, shaking each one's hand and giving Grace a gentle hug. When he got to Connie, he said, "And lovely to see you again, Connie."

Connie handed Damian the box she was carrying. "Thank you again for supporting our nutrition center project. Here are the candy cane earrings you ordered for the cast." He had already given Connie a check when he placed his order.

Damian took the box and handed it to a servant. "Anything for Concetta's niece. Ernest, put these on a nice tray for when we give them out later."

Ernest took the box and disappeared into what Connie assumed was the kitchen, since two servers in black tuxedos, each with a tray of hors d'oeuvres, had just emerged from its doorway.

Connie scanned the marble-tiled room. There were about a hundred party-goers exuding elegance and milling about between the spacious living room and the lanai. The temperature was in the low seventies and the bi-folding living room doors were wide open, allowing a fresh, salty breeze to fill the house. Guests spilled from the living room to the expansive lanai, and although it was dark, softly crashing waves revealed that the Gulf of Mexico was only a short distance beyond it. Christmas music streamed through a sound system as laughter and friendly banter came from various corners of the room.

It had all the makings of a spectacular party.

Chapter 3

"WE ARE THRILLED that you could share this night with us," Damian said to Connie and her group.

"And it means so much to all of us that you will be present at opening night tomorrow," Sophie added.

The servers carrying trays with various appetizers made their way around the room. When the tray of chicken wings arrived at Connie's group, a little boy in a light gray suit and red shirt left the group he was standing with, which consisted of two other children and several adults, and stood between Connie and Damian. The fact that he only had eyes for the tray of food told Connie he had come over to get seconds on the chicken wings.

Damian laughed and tousled the boy's messy bleach blond hair. "We ordered the chicken wings for the children in the play. This is Stevie Lambert. He's playing the role of Tiny Tim in tomorrow's production."

"Nice to meet you, Stevie," Connie said. "How old are you?"

"Seven."

A woman in a hunter green dress with thick wavy brown hair and friendly green eyes came and stood behind Stevie, placing her hands on his shoulders.

As the woman approached their group, Sophie took a protective step closer to her husband.

"Stevie, save some wings for everyone one else," the woman said, looking slightly uncomfortable.

"Nonsense," Damian said, bending until he was eye level with the child. "Stevie, you take as many as you want."

"What do you say to Mr. Pritchard?" the woman asked.

"Thank you," Stevie said with a wide grin.

"I'm Eloise Lambert, or better known around here as Stevie's mom," she said.

Damian chuckled. "Eloise is being modest. She is a wonderful actress, and her son has inherited her ability."

Stevie beamed as he smiled at his mother.

Eloise winked at her son.

Pulling a roll of antacid from his pant pocket, Damian popped a couple tablets into his mouth.

"Are you still taking those things?" Grace asked.

He waved her off. "Yes, pay no attention to me. It's just a recurring little problem that comes and goes. I've grown accustomed to dealing with it."

Eloise shook her head. "He's been popping those antacid pills for as long as we've known each other, and we go way back. But it seems to be getting worse lately."

Sophie's shoulders stiffened.

"Nonsense," Damian said. "About my taking more antacid tablets, that is. It is true that Eloise and I have known each other for years. She was one of our best actresses at the Sapphire Beach Playhouse until she got pregnant with Stevie."

"Yes, then my husband Stephen and I decided I'd stay home to raise Stevie until he went to school. But I've gotten so involved in volunteer activities and such that I decided to put off going back to work."

Stephen is out of town for business for the week, or he'd be here tonight," Eloise said, glancing at Sophie.

When they finished chatting, Damian and Sophie excused themselves, and Connie and her group decided to get some fresh air on the lanai, where many of the guests had congregated.

"I'll meet you out there," Connie said. "I want to find a restroom first."

Connie looked around for Damian or Sophie to ask where it was located, but she didn't see Sophie, and Damian was in the middle of a conversation. So, after noticing a couple of people coming down the hallway, Connie guessed that the restroom must be in that direction.

She went to open the first door she came to, but when she started to open it, the abrupt sound of Sophie's voice startled her. "What are you looking for?"

Connie jumped and turned her head at the sound of Sophie's voice.

Sophie pulled Connie's hand away from the doorknob, which appeared to be locked, anyway.

"The restroom is over there," she said, pointing to a door on the opposite side of the hallway. Then, regaining her composure, she said, "Sorry to startle you. It's just that this is a guest room, and it's a complete mess right now. I'd be mortified if anyone saw it."

"Sorry about that," Connie said. "I understand." At least she *partly* understood. It seemed like an inappropriately strong reaction to an innocent mistake.

A few minutes later, on her way to join the others on the lanai, Connie stopped to admire the largest Christmas tree she had ever seen in a private residence. It had to be fifteen feet high and was decorated in white lights and designer ornaments. Connie preferred more of a mix of store-bought and homemade Christmas ornaments, but she couldn't argue that this tree was something to behold. She finally peeled her eyes off the tree and made her way to the lanai.

When she rejoined her group, the women were talking to a man named William Deveaux, who looked slightly bored. William turned out to be Damian's understudy.

"Damian hasn't taken on any roles lately, since he has had his hands full with the administrative aspects of the operation. But he wanted to come out of retirement, so-to-speak, for this play. I guess it has sentimental value because of Concetta."

"That was very kind of him," Grace said. "We appreciate that you are dedicating this play to her memory."

"Everyone loved Concetta. In addition to having been an amazing actress, she also had quite the gift for fundraising."

Connie smiled knowingly. "I know what you mean. I used to work for a humanitarian organization, and Concetta had a knack for getting people to donate to a worthy cause."

"She sure did," William said. "Since she passed away, donations to the playhouse have been significantly lower."

"I'm sorry to hear that," Gianna said. "I hope that this play helps to get things back on track."

"We all do," William said. "None of us wants the playhouse to close. We even used to bring in talent from New York for some of our bigger productions, but those days are gone." William motioned to a woman across the room. "Please excuse me," he said. "I think my wife needs me to bail her out of a boring conversation."

"My goodness," Jo said after William left. "I had no idea the playhouse was in danger of closing. I know Concetta did a lot of fundraising, but I didn't realize things were this bad."

"I wonder if that's why Damian's been taking more antacid lately," Stephanie said.

"It would be a terrible shame if the playhouse closed," Grace said. "Concetta was passionate about this theatre. She not only loved the productions, but there is also an educational arm to the organization, and some of the actors even direct plays at the local high school or offer free classes to children in the area as part of the mission."

"Excuse me," came a male voice from behind Connie. "Did I hear you talking about Concetta Belmonte?"

Connie turned around to discover a distinguished-looking man with light eyes and dark hair, graying around the temples, accompanied by a woman in a sleeveless A-line navy dress with blond hair that went halfway down her back.

"Yes, she was my sister. I'm Josephine Petretta and these are my daughters, Connie and Gianna. This is Concetta's best friend, Grace, and two close friends, Elyse and Stephanie."

"Of course. How are you Grace?" the man asked.

"Aside from missing my friend, I'm doing well, Rick."

"Yes, we miss Concetta dearly. She was an institution around the Sapphire Beach Playhouse," the woman said.

"It's a pleasure to meet you all," Rick said to the others, flashing a charming smile. "I'm Rick Bennett, the director of 'A Christmas Carol,' and this is my wife, Priscilla."

"It's lovely to meet you," Jo said. "We are looking forward to tomorrow evening's production."

"I hope this is not inappropriate," Rick said to Jo, "But while I have you here, if you ever come across a key to the playhouse, we would love to have it back. They are special keys and rather expensive to duplicate."

"You can ask my daughter about that," Jo said, gesturing to Connie. "She lives is Concetta's condo now."

"I did find a few keys I didn't recognize when I was cleaning it out, so I put them in the junk drawer," Connie said. "I'll check for you."

Rick pulled a key from his pocket and held it up. "It would look like this."

Connie examined the key. "I'll check the drawer and see if it's in there."

Rick thanked her and gave her his phone number so she could contact him if she found it. "It would be much appreciated."

Just then, Damian's commanding voice drifted onto the lanai from the living room. "May I have everyone's attention?"

The guests migrated to the living room to hear him better.

As Damian spoke, the crowd grew quiet. "Sophie and I wanted to welcome you to our home for our tenth annual Sapphire Beach Playhouse Christmas party. It is wonderful to be able to gather outside of work to enjoy one another's company. I also wanted to thank everyone for all the hard work you have put into this year's Christmas production, which, as you know, is being dedicated to the memory of Concetta Belmonte, whom we all knew and loved." The guests erupted in applause. "In case you haven't yet had a chance to meet them, some of Concetta's loved ones are here tonight." He raised his hand toward Connie's group. "In fact, I'd like to invite Concetta's niece, Connie, to come forward."

Connie looked at Jo and Gianna and they both shrugged. She went over to stand near Damian while he told the crowd about *Just Jewelry* and the store's Fair Trade section, encouraging them to stop by to do some Christmas shopping. Then he invited Connie to explain about the chicken coop project in Kenya, which she happily did.

After Connie's explanation, Damian announced that he had purchased a pair of candy cane earrings for the cast and crew of 'A Christmas Carol,' and invited Connie to hand them out, while her mother, sister, and friends assisted her. Everyone was delighted at Damian's gesture. Those not involved in the play promised to visit the store and support the fundraiser.

Damian continued, "I purchased enough for the entire cast and crew, even the men. Gentlemen, please give yours to someone special. You can even tell your sweetheart that you bought it for her as a

Christmas present. I promise I won't tell. Except you, Stevie. You're too young to have a sweetheart."

When they finished distributing the earrings. Jo squeezed Connie's shoulder. "It seems my sister's fundraising efforts have continued even beyond her death."

Connie smiled. "I was thinking the same thing."

After Damian's introduction, the women suddenly became popular. They mingled and met various people, who talked of their love for Concetta and promised to stop by *Just Jewelry*. Soon it was getting late, and the women decided it was time to go home. Between work and the play, Connie would have a long day tomorrow, and she was certain that Hannah and Noah would wake her sister up early, as well.

So, finally around midnight, they left.

***

Connie's alarm went off on Friday morning mere seconds after her head hit the pillow. Or at least it felt that way. After kicking off the sheets and dragging herself out of bed, Connie made breakfast, took Ginger for a quick walk along the boulevard, then headed into the store to get ready for a busy day. Fortunately, Gianna was occupying the twins, so she was able to make a quick getaway.

The first thing Connie noticed when she arrived at the shop was a basket on the table filled with candy cane earrings. Abby and the jewelry-making class had come through!

Connie counted fifty pairs, which did more for her energy level than her morning coffee had done. After Damian's purchase of twenty-five, and the others that had already been made, Connie calculated that they had about a hundred more to make. There was light at the end of the tunnel.

Connie had insisted that Grace take the day off, since she had a longer-than-usual day on Wednesday, the day Connie's family arrived. Abby would be there at 4:00 so that both Connie and Grace could attend the opening of the play.

The day passed quickly, and before Connie knew it, Abby had arrived.

"I hope I'm not working you too hard," Connie said. She hadn't intended on having Abby work the store alone when she hired her, but she proved herself more than capable. Besides, Abby would be going home for Christmas break a week from Monday, so Connie wanted to take advantage of her availability while she could.

"Are you kidding? I love it here, and I'm a poor student who needs the money. Especially at Christmastime."

Connie laughed. "Well, you certainly have been a lifesaver."

She spent a half hour with Abby before heading home to get ready for the play.

The women once again met in the lobby of Palm Paradise so they could arrive at the playhouse together. Connie couldn't wait to see the play. It was not only one of Concetta's favorites, but it was one of Connie's, as well.

They arrived at the theatre with plenty of time to spare. Connie handed their tickets to a friendly usher with short dark hair sprayed firmly into place, who was wearing a pair of Connie's candy cane earrings. She sported a hunter green blazer that was embroidered with the Sapphire Beach Playhouse logo and held a black flashlight at her side with one hand while she examined the tickets in the other.

"You have fantastic seats," the woman said.

"We are so grateful," Connie said. "The play is being done in honor of my Aunt Concetta, who was Chair of the Board of Directors before she passed away." Connie introduced the others in her group.

The woman put her hand on her heart. "I am so happy to meet you. My name is Dottie McKenzie. I have volunteered as an usher for years, and Concetta was the most down-to-earth person in this whole place. She was my favorite celebrity, except for Damian Pritchard, of course."

Dottie went on to gush over Damian until Connie finally managed to change the subject by commenting on the woman's earrings. "You look familiar," Connie said. "You must have bought your pair of earrings in my shop, *Just Jewelry*. Perhaps we met when you purchased it."

"Ah, yes," Dottie said. "The display in the window with the sign about the chicken coop project caught my attention. I bought one for myself and a few for the girls. That's what I call my close friends. We always meet for dinner around Christmastime to exchange gifts, and these will be perfect. They will love both the earrings and the fact that they are for a good cause."

Connie thanked Dottie for her patronage, and the women slid into their front-row seats.

While they were waiting for the show to begin, Grace called their attention to a two-page spread in the beginning of the program, which had a picture of Concetta, along with a beautiful tribute highlighting both her career as an actress and her contributions to the playhouse. A feeling of nostalgia came over Connie as she looked at her aunt's picture.

While they waited for the play to begin, the women chatted about the things they would do over the next couple of weeks. Connie was so wrapped up in their conversation that she didn't realize it was 7:05 until Elyse mentioned it.

"I wonder what could be holding up the performance?" Elyse asked.

"Plays always begin at least five minutes late," Grace assured her. "They want to make sure everyone has arrived and is seated before starting."

After ten more minutes, murmuring began among the audience.

Jo turned and scanned the crowd. "I think people are beginning to notice the time."

Connie looked around for Dottie to see if she knew what was going on but was unable to locate her.

"There seems to be a lot of scurrying around back there," Grace said. "Why don't we go see what's happening? I've been backstage enough with Concetta to know my way around."

"I'm coming," Jo and Gianna said in unison.

"Stephanie and I can wait here so there aren't too many of us," Elyse said.

Stephanie nodded her agreement. "Text us if there's any news."

Connie, Jo, Gianna, and Grace discretely made their way backstage. Since they had been at the party the night before and knew some of the cast, Connie hoped they would blend in with the others.

There was so much activity that nobody even noticed them.

"The twins would love it back here," Gianna said. "With all these curtains, they could have quite a game of Hide and Seek."

The first person they recognized was Eloise Lambert. She had her arm around Stevie and appeared concerned.

"Eloise, do you know what the holdup is?"

"We are waiting for Damian to emerge from his dressing room so the play can begin. He was feeling nauseous and lightheaded earlier, so Rick went in a while ago to check on him, but he hasn't returned yet."

As if on cue, Rick appeared. He looked paler than the Ghost of Christmas past.

"What's happening, Rick?" William asked. "What's the delay?"

"This time, I don't think the show will go on," Rick said, barely able to get out the words. "Damian Pritchard is dead."

Chapter 4

CONNIE FUMBLED FOR HER PHONE, and with quivering fingers, shot off a text to Elyse to inform her and Stephanie of Damian's death.

I'm leaving the theatre right now, Elyse replied. *Josh is watching the girls, and he'll want to be here. Stephanie's going backstage to be with her mother.*

It was like watching a scene from a movie unfold before her eyes. Connie shook her head to clear the fog and regain focus. It suddenly occurred to her that Sophie was not among them. Did she even know that her husband had died?

Grace must have read her mind. "Where's Sophie?" she asked.

"She was the first to find Damian's body," Rick said. "She was in his dressing room sobbing when I got there. I found a couple of her friends to take her to another room and stay with her. That's what took me so long."

While they waited for the police to arrive, Connie observed each person's reaction to the news of Damian's death, just in case the information would be useful later. It was possible that Damian died of natural causes. People unexpectedly passed away every day from hidden health issues. As far as she knew, he didn't have any life-threatening concerns, so foul play was at least a possibility.

Everyone, without exception, genuinely appeared to be in shock. But, then again, she was looking at a cast of actors, so of course they would all *appear* innocent. Appearances were their livelihood.

"I want to get Stevie out of here," Eloise said.

Connie placed a hand on her forearm. "I'm sorry, but I think you'll have to stick around. The police will want to question everyone when they arrive."

Eloise gasped. "The police? Are you saying you think there was foul play involved?"

"I'm not saying that. But as far as we know Damian didn't have any life-threatening illnesses, so the police will likely treat it as a suspicious death until they know more."

"Connie's right," Rick said. "I'll make an announcement that the show is cancelled."

William looked confused. "What do you mean cancelled? The show can still go on. I'm prepared to play the part of Scrooge."

Those around him just stared at him, dumbfounded.

"Your friend and colleague was just murdered, and the Sapphire Beach Playhouse could potentially become a crime scene. I think it's safe to say that tonight's performance is cancelled," Grace said in a tone one would use to reprimand a young child.

Rick headed toward the curtain leading to the stage, but Connie grabbed his arm to stop him from making the announcement. "I wouldn't do that quite yet. We don't know if the police will want to question anyone in the audience. I would let them decide who to dismiss and when."

Unfortunately, due to some recent experiences with murder investigations, Connie wasn't unfamiliar with basic crime scene procedure.

"Good point," Rick said. "I'll just announce that there will be a delay in tonight's performance."

While Rick made the announcement, Connie whispered to Grace, "Do you know where Damian's dressing room is?"

"Yes, I think I can find it."

The two women disappeared before anyone could stop them. But since everyone was preoccupied with the tragic news, nobody seemed to notice when they slipped away, including Jo and Gianna. They peered into a few empty rooms, and when they came across a closed door, Grace tugged on Connie's arm. "I think this is the one."

With Grace hovering close behind her, Connie slowly opened the door and found Damian Pritchard lying lifeless on the floor.

"It looks like he just collapsed," Grace whispered. "I don't see any blood or weapon."

Connie scanned the room for any clues that might reveal what happened. Two water glasses had been left on the vanity, one with red lipstick, and an opened bottle of antacid with some of the chalky white liquid dripping down the side, sat a couple of feet away, also on the vanity. Connie's heart sank when she spotted a candy cane earring on the floor next to Damian's body.

Judging from Grace's expression, she must have noticed the earring about the same time as Connie did.

Connie cautiously entered the dressing room.

"Don't touch anything," Grace said.

"I know. I won't." Even with his stage makeup applied, Damian's face appeared pale, and there was some foaming around his mouth. "I smell bitter almonds."

"Connie! What are you doing?" Her mother's shrill tone made her feel like a teenager who just got busted for something she knew she shouldn't be doing.

She turned around to find her mother, Gianna, and Stephanie looking curiously at her. "I don't want you getting involved in this, Connie," her mother said. "Don't you encourage her, Grace."

Grace shrugged. "Believe me, Jo, I've tried to keep her out of these things before but as you can see, I've given up."

"If you can't beat 'em, join 'em," Gianna said, plowing past Grace.

"Don't disturb anything," Connie said, before pointing out the earring.

The commotion in the area where members of the cast and crew were gathered told Connie that the police had arrived. The four women scooted out and found a police officer and two EMTs from Sapphire Beach Fire Rescue talking with the actors. Then they all dashed out back to Damian's dressing room.

Sergeant Tim Donohue was the next to arrive on the scene, followed a few minutes later by Zach and Josh. They were the only two detectives in the Sapphire Beach Police Department, so Connie wasn't surprised that they both showed up.

Zach came over to where Connie, Jo, Gianna, Stephanie, and Grace were standing. "I almost forgot that tonight's show was dedicated in memory of your aunt," he said to Connie.

Connie revealed what she knew, leaving out her own mini-inspection of the crime scene. "By the way," Connie added when she finished, "this is my mom, Jo, and my sister, Gianna. Mom, Gi, this is Zach."

It wasn't how she envisioned her mother and sister meeting Zach, but truth be told, it kind of took the pressure off. She wasn't exactly sure how to introduce him, and she didn't want her family to create an awkward situation by making too big a deal out of their relationship, so this worked out perfectly. Well... except for the murder.

"It's lovely to meet you, Zach," Jo said, a wide grin spreading across her face. "We've heard so much about you. I do hope we will see you again soon under better circumstances. Perhaps you could come to the house for Christmas dinner?"

Connie's cheeks grew warm. She had totally planned on reaching out to him to extend the invitation herself. After all, Zach didn't have any family in Sapphire Beach. Josh was his best friend, and he and Elyse had already agreed to come. But it was still a little awkward that her mother took the liberty of inviting him.

Connie's eyes met Zach's questioning glance.

"Of course, you are welcome, Zach. I had planned to invite you, but it looks like my mother beat me to it. Josh, Elyse, and the girls will be coming, as well."

He smiled warmly. "I appreciate the invitation. I'll be there."

Zach glanced over at Sergeant Donovan, who had his hands full interviewing witnesses. "I'd better go."

By the time the women talked to the police and were able to leave the theatre, it was after 10:00. The forensic investigators were still at work, and much of the theatre was being treated as a crime scene. Connie overheard Sergeant Donovan telling Zach that the surveillance cameras hadn't been working for a while, so they would be of no help. They were on the list of items needing to be repaired, but unfortunately, there was no money in the budget to fix them.

As they drove home, there were two questions that weighed heavily on Connie's mind. *Did Damian Pritchard die of natural causes, or was there foul play involved?* And *What was one of my candy cane earrings doing next to his body?*

When they returned to Palm Paradise, everyone gathered in Connie's living room, including Grace and Stephanie. Although it had been an exhausting evening, nobody seemed quite ready to call it a night. Ginger hopped onto Connie's lap, and she stroked the dog's silky fur.

The women filled Greg and Gary in on what happened in more detail and described what they saw in Damian's dressing room.

Jo hung her head. "It's just hitting me that a man was murdered at what was supposed to be a tribute to my sister. Concetta would be devastated if she were alive to see this."

Grace put her arm around Jo's shoulders.

It hurt Connie's heart to see her mother so upset.

"You ladies were at the Christmas party at Damian's house last night," Greg said. "Did you notice anything out of the ordinary with Damian or any of the guests?"

"Aside from popping antacid pills like they were candy, Damian appeared healthy," Gianna said, looking to the others to see if they agreed.

Connie, Jo, Grace, Elyse, and Stephanie all nodded in agreement.

"He was well-liked as far as I could tell," Jo said.

"Maybe his heartburn wasn't heartburn at all. It could have been a symptom of heart disease," Greg said. "He probably had a heart attack."

"Normally I would agree," Connie said. "But I specifically remember Eloise saying that he had had this problem for many years. If it was a heart condition, it would have killed him long before tonight."

"What I want to know," Grace said, "is what one of our candy cane earrings was doing next to the body."

"Let's just say for the sake of argument that Damian was killed," Connie said.

Greg opened his mouth to object, but Connie cut him off. "Just humor me, Dad. The other actors said he seemed fine when he arrived at the theatre two hours before. So, he must have gotten suddenly ill. And there was a faint scent of almonds near the body. I did a quick search on my phone while we were waiting for the police to dismiss us, and that could indicate cyanide poisoning. If Damian was poisoned, the earring could belong to the killer."

"But Damian gave a pair of candy cane earrings to the entire cast and crew at the party last night," Gianna said. "If it was indeed the killer who left the earring at the crime scene, it could have been anyone connected to the play."

"Or anyone else who bought a pair of those earrings at *Just Jewelry*," Grace said. "We haven't sold a ton yet, but, in addition to the twenty-five that Damian purchased, we have probably sold about twenty more."

"That would mean the killer is a woman," Jo said.

Greg looked at Gary and shook his head. "What killer? The police haven't even determined that it was a homicide."

"That doesn't mean anything," Connie said. "All suspicious deaths have to be treated as homicides. That's why the detectives and forensic investigators came tonight. The toxicology report can take four to six weeks to come back, so the police can't wait to receive the results before they begin investigating."

Greg ran a hand through his thick graying brown hair. "Connie, it scares me that you know these things. This proves that you've been involved in too many murder investigations since moving to Sapphire Beach."

"I'm not getting involved in anything," Connie said. "I'm just discussing what we know."

"Just promise me that's as far as it goes. All of you," Greg said, waving his finger at each of them.

Jo ignored her husband's request. "I did notice the usher who seated us was wearing a pair of candy cane earrings."

"Yes, I noticed that too," Connie said. "Her name was Dottie McKenzie."

"I doubt ushers have access backstage," Stephanie said.

"Good point," Gianna said. "So basically, the killer is likely a woman who was at Damian's Christmas party, or who bought the earrings from *Just Jewelry*, and had backstage access. That doesn't narrow things down very much."

"*If* there was a killer," Gary said. "It's just as likely that Damian had a disease he didn't know about."

"Or one he knew about but didn't tell anyone," Greg added.

"I went back to see Sophie and offer my condolences," Grace said. "As far as she knew, Damian was healthy."

"I don't envy the work that the police have ahead of them," Stephanie said.

"Finally, a sensible statement," Greg said. "*The police* have a lot of work ahead of them. The guys that are paid and trained to hunt down killers."

The women once again ignored Greg's observation, and each seemed lost in thought.

"If he was poisoned," Gianna said, "it would have to have been someone close to him."

"And the person would have needed access to his food or beverages," Connie said.

Greg glanced at the clock on the DVR. "I can see this is a losing battle. It's getting late, and I'm beat. I think I'll call it a night."

"I'll be right behind you," Jo said. "I'm just going to have some herbal tea before bed."

Connie jumped up. "I just remembered I haven't walked Ginger yet."

"It's late," Gary said. "I'll do it."

"Thanks, Gary. That's why you're my favorite brother-in-law," she said playfully.

"I'll take the compliment, even though I'm your *only* brother-in-law."

"It's been a long day," Stephanie said. "I should go, too. I'll walk down with you."

Once everyone had left, Connie, Jo, and Gianna were alone.

"So, what's our plan, Detective Connie?" Gianna asked.

"Well, I hate to say it, but Dad's right. We shouldn't insert ourselves into a police investigation."

Jo looked at Connie with raised eyebrows. "Who are you, and what have you done with my daughter?"

Connie tried to suppress a smirk. "But that doesn't mean we can't pose a few strategic questions. After all, Damian and Auntie Concetta were good friends, so it would be strange if we weren't at least curious. They'll probably reschedule the performance soon. Let's see what we can learn when we go back to the theatre."

Chapter 5

ON SATURDAY MORNING, Connie and Gianna persuaded their father to make pancakes, eggs, and bacon. Since Jo was an amazing cook, Greg never had any incentive to develop his own skills, which left a lot to be desired when it came to dinner, but his pancakes could rival the best breakfast joints.

"What's on the agenda for today?" Connie asked after they said grace. Her mouth watered as she piled bacon, eggs, and three fluffy golden brown pancakes on her plate and covered them with butter and maple syrup.

"We thought we'd spend the day on the beach," Gianna said. "Gary and I are determined not to leave Florida without a tan, and the kids have their hearts set on building sandcastles."

"I was hoping we could rent a pontoon boat one day, like we did a few years ago," Jo said.

Connie smiled as she remembered their trip to Sapphire Beach the year before the twins were born, when the whole family, including Concetta, spent the afternoon gliding across the Gulf of Mexico. "I'm in, as long as I can get the time off from work," Connie said. "And feel free to use my new paddleboard today. It's in the storage closet in the garage."

Connie walked Ginger while the others cleaned up after breakfast, then headed into the shop. She had been missing her sidekick at *Just Jewelry*, so she decided to take Ginger with her for the day. Besides, she suspected the poor little dog needed a respite from her three-year-old playmates.

Connie barely arrived at *Just Jewelry* in time to open the store at 9:00. She had told Grace to take her time coming in, since they had had a late night at the theatre. Connie got to work right away creating more candy cane earrings, in between serving customers. She hated to think that one of her earrings was found next to Damian's body, but she refused to let that put a damper on the fundraiser. The nutrition center project was too important.

An hour later, Grace arrived with two coffees in hand. "I thought after last night and a house full of company, you could use an extra caffeine boost," she said, handing one of the coffees to Connie.

"Thank you, Grace. But you are in the same boat with my parents staying at your house."

Grace laughed. "Your parents are easy compared to two three-year-olds."

The mention of the twins brought a smile to Connie's face. "I'm relishing every moment with them. Being in their everyday life is what I miss most about living so far from Boston. But I'm not going to lie," Connie said, after taking a long sip of coffee. "They are a handful."

For the rest of the morning, Grace tended to the customers while Connie continued to work on the earrings. Just as she and Grace were about to take a break, Zach stopped in.

"I wanted to make sure everyone is okay," he said, sitting across from Connie and Grace at the oak table where Connie had been working. "Your poor family. They came to Sapphire Beach early to attend a play and honor your aunt's memory, and opening night is cancelled for a tragedy."

Connie noticed that Zach didn't use the word murder.

"We had such a wonderful time at Damian's Christmas party," Connie said, thinking back to the Gulf-front mansion exquisitely decorated for the festive occasion and the hospitality they had received. "It was so nice to be back in Concetta's world with my mother and sister. We are devastated that this happened in my aunt's beloved theatre. She used to refer to the Sapphire Beach Playhouse as her pet project."

"I'm sorry this has been so hard," Zach said.

"I know you have to treat all suspicious deaths as potential homicides, but do you think Damian really was murdered?" Connie asked.

"All we can do is speculate. From the appearance of the body and from what the Medical Examiner said last night, the preliminary signs point to poison. But we won't receive the toxicology report for at least a month. In the meantime, we are treating it as a homicide investigation."

"If it was murder, the faster you get it solved, the better chance the playhouse has of surviving. I imagine they will lose money from cancelling last night's performance."

"The forensic investigators finished processing the scene this morning, so the opening performance has been rescheduled for tonight. They are going to add a couple of extra shows for those who were planning to attend last night's and this afternoon's performances. They'll still lose a little money, but it won't be as bad as it could have been."

A lump grew in Connie's throat. The Sapphire Beach Playhouse couldn't afford to lose even a penny, if things were as bad as William had said.

"The other actors said Damian was fine when he arrived at the theatre at 5:00, and they didn't think he ate anything while he was there. What could he have ingested that contained poison?" Connie snapped her fingers. "The antacid! It was common knowledge that Damian consumed a large amount of antacid before every show. I'll bet his antacid bottle was laced with cyanide."

"Woah, Sherlock, slow down," Zach said, laughing. "We sent everything in the dressing room to the lab, so if your theory is true, we'll know soon enough."

"And what about the candy cane earring? Somebody wearing a pair of my earrings was clearly in his dressing room last night. Since Damian gave a pair to the entire cast and crew on Thursday night, the killer was likely someone who was at the Christmas party."

"I'm not going to ask how you knew there was a candy cane earring at the crime scene," Zach said. "But yes, that's one possible scenario. We are just in the beginning stages of our investigation. Speaking of which, I have to get back to work. I just wanted to check in. And thanks again for the invitation to Christmas dinner."

Shortly after Zach left, Connie received an email from the theatre informing her that the performance had been rescheduled for that evening at 7:00.

"Damian would have wanted the show to go on," Grace said, when Connie informed her. "The cast and crew worked so hard on this play and the Sapphire Beach community deserves a Christmas production. I'm glad the play is on."

Connie texted the others, and they made plans to attend opening night for the second time.

While Grace tended to some customers, Connie opened her laptop and performed a more extensive internet search for cyanide poisoning than she had been able to do the previous night at the theatre. Based on everything she knew – what Eloise had said about Damian complaining of nausea and dizziness before he died, plus his pale skin and the bitter almond smell near the body - Connie was more convinced than ever that Damian had been poisoned by cyanide. Her research told her that a high enough dose could kill someone within fifteen minutes.

Since there would be a performance that evening, Connie figured that at least some of the cast and crew would be at the theatre tidying up after the police. It might be a good opportunity to ask some questions. Grace agreed to cover the store while Connie went to the theatre, but not before Connie promised to pick up lunch on the way back.

When Connie arrived at the theatre, the actors were milling about, some eating and others relaxing. Rick was sitting in the front row. He seemed to be taking a break, so Connie took a seat next to him.

She shivered as she realized that she had been sitting in almost the same seat last night while Damian was dying.

"How are you doing?" Connie asked.

Rick shrugged. "I called a last-minute rehearsal to get everyone's head back in the game. Everyone's shaken up from Damian's death, of course, but we'll pull off the show. It's a cast of professionals." He nodded toward Stevie, who was eating lunch with his mother on the other side of the theatre. "Even Stevie is rising to the occasion."

Connie smiled and waved at them.

"I just keep thinking how devastated my aunt would be if she were alive."

Rick nodded. "You're right. She loved the playhouse, and she considered Damian a friend."

"Judging from the questions the police were asking, it sounds like they suspect foul play," Connie said. "If that's true, do you have any idea who might have wanted to harm Damian?"

Rick leaned back in his seat, staring at the curtain in front of him. "The Sapphire Beach Playhouse has its share of drama." He turned toward Connie with a smirk. "No pun intended. Perhaps a crazy fan did it."

Then he turned his gaze toward Eloise. "Or someone connected with the play."

Connie followed Rick's gaze to where Eloise was sitting. "Why would Eloise want to harm Damian?" Connie asked in a whispered tone. "Damian seemed to have a lot of respect for both Eloise and Stevie."

"Let's just say she and Damian... have a history. A *long* history. They worked together in California before she even came to Sapphire Beach." Rick leaned closer to Connie. "And just between you and me, things were rocky between Sophie and Damian. There was a rumor that Damian was going to move out after the Christmas party."

"You know how people talk here," Connie said. "The separation could just be a rumor."

Rick shrugged. "It's possible. But if you ask me, Damian did everything in his power to keep Eloise around the playhouse and as close to him as possible. He even used Stevie, giving him various roles. Lucky for all of us, Stevie takes after his mother and can act. Nobody really complained because Stevie was good, but if he wasn't, we'd all be in trouble."

It was interesting information, but it still didn't make sense. If they were in a romantic relationship, why would Eloise want to hurt Damian? If Eloise's husband suspected an affair between Damian and his wife, he certainly would have a motive for murder. But Stephen was out of town last night.

Connie glanced over at Eloise and Stevie, then back at Rick. "I'd like to chat with them. Is there time before rehearsal begins again?"

"Go ahead. You have a few minutes."

Connie approached Eloise and Stevie, who were finishing their sandwiches. "I just stopped by to offer my condolences," Connie said. Then to Stevie, she said, "I'll be at opening night tonight and can't wait to see you as Tiny Tim."

"Stevie," Eloise said, "why don't you go wash your hands before rehearsal begins again?"

"How's he holding up?" Connie asked once Stevie was out of earshot.

"He's sad. Damian was good to him. But I'm trying to keep his mind on the show. Neither Stevie nor the other child actors know that the police suspect foul play. But the rest of us know because of the questions they asked us last night. Everyone has been great about making sure that the kids don't find out unless their parents choose to tell them. We just told Stevie that Damian was sick and passed away unexpectedly."

"That seems wise," Connie said. "Damian seemed like a lovely man. He went out of his way to make my family and me feel welcome at his home during the Christmas party. It's hard to imagine anyone wanting to hurt him. You've known him for a long time. Do you know if he had any enemies?"

Eloise smirked. "Damian Pritchard was a charming and gracious man. He was larger than life at times and he had a good heart. But when he wanted something, he would do anything in his power to get it."

Connie looked straight into Eloise's eyes. "Some say that *you* were one of the things he would do anything to get."

Eloise pulled back and put her hand on her chest.

"I'm happily married, Connie, and Damian was married to a wonderful woman. As far as I'm concerned, that option wasn't even on the table." Eloise looked around nervously. Connie wondered if she was watching out for Stevie or trying to make sure that nobody else overheard their conversation. She continued, "Many people didn't agree with

Damian's approach to running this playhouse, so there's that. He had some difficult decisions to make, and some people feared for their jobs. Plus, as I said, he was a very charming man with a lot of female fans who were really into him. He was a local celebrity and even had to be careful when he went out. Maybe one of them was a little too obsessed."

Connie thought about what Eloise said. If Eloise was right, that added to the number of possible motives. "Is there any fan in particular that comes to mind?"

Just then, Rick announced that they would be starting up rehearsals again in two minutes.

Eloise looked around. "I don't see Stevie. I need to make sure he's on time. But there is one woman who volunteers as an usher: Dottie McKenzie. She was gaga over Damian."

Dottie had been on Connie's list of suspects, since she been wearing candy cane earrings, but she wouldn't have had backstage access. "The killer would have had to have been backstage," Connie said. "I thought ushers aren't permitted back there."

"Permitted or not," Eloise said, "I saw Dottie backstage on opening night about twenty minutes before the play was due to start. She must have snuck backstage in between seating people. It wasn't the first time she tried to see Damian before a show. It's like she thought she was a member the cast. If you ask me, she was delusional. She would even want to wish Damian luck when he wasn't performing. She would say that his hard work made every performance possible. It used to annoy him to no end. She was warned that if she did it one more time, she would be asked not to return as an usher."

That would have put Dottie backstage just after she seated Connie and her group. Given the timeline that Connie had pieced together, it was possible that Damian was poisoned right around that time.

Chapter 6

ON SATURDAY EVENING, Connie arranged to meet the others at the theatre so she could arrive early to talk with Dottie.

But Jo and Gianna quickly figured out Connie's scheme and refused to let her go alone.

"I'm not going to miss a chance to see my sister the sleuth at work," Gianna said.

They arrived about 6:15 so they could catch Dottie alone. Sure enough, they found her milling about in the lobby admiring the Christmas tree, which was decorated with pinecones and Christmas berry branches.

"Good evening," Dottie said. "You're Concetta's family, aren't you? Can I take you to your seats?"

Connie glanced at Dottie's ears and noticed she was wearing pearl earrings and not the candy cane earrings that she had on yesterday. Had she lost one at the crime scene, or did she just choose not to wear them that night?

"I think we're all set," Connie replied. "We have the same seats that we had last night, and I think I remember how to get there. Besides, I'd like to stand for a few minutes since we'll be seated for the performance."

"I don't blame you. Please let me know if you change your mind, and I'll be happy to walk you down."

Dottie started to leave, but Connie stopped her. "Dottie, I noticed you're not wearing your candy cane earrings tonight. I hope you didn't lose one?"

Dottie nervously touched her ears. "Um, no, they are at home. I just decided to wear a different pair tonight instead."

Connie smiled. "They are lovely. With everything that's been going on, I admire you all for pulling together and doing the play, despite last night's tragedy."

Dottie nodded solemnly.

74

"I know you were a big fan of Damian as an actor, but did you know him well?" Connie asked.

Dottie stared at the ground as if she were pondering the question. "I considered him a good friend."

If what Eloise said was true, Damian didn't return the sentiment.

"Are you friends with his wife, Sophie, as well?" Connie asked. "I met her at a party. She seems like a lovely woman."

At the mention of Sophie's name, Dottie looked as though she had been punched in the stomach. "I'm sure she's very kind. I never met her."

Jo, apparently getting into the spirit of interviewing Dottie, decided to chime in. "Damian was a very handsome man. You know, if I wasn't a married woman…"

Connie and Gianna exchanged a surprised glance. Connie really hoped her mother was bluffing.

To Connie's relief, Jo winked at her daughters while Dottie was looking away.

Jo's instigation seemed to have done the trick. Dottie's hands flew onto her hips. "Well, you would have to have gotten in line." There was a bitter edge in her tone. "I'll bet Sophie knew that she had some competition. I've been thinking about this since last night. If Damian was going to leave her, and rumor had it that he was, maybe she killed him so nobody else could have him, or so she could inherit all his money instead of ending up with just an alimony check."

Was Dottie implying that Damian was going to leave Sophie for *her*? They couldn't be more different. Maybe Eloise was right. Dottie was delusional.

"That's an interesting theory," Connie said. "I understand that you were seen backstage before the performance. May I ask what you were doing there? As far as I know, ushers don't normally wander backstage."

Dottie's lower lip trembled. "I just went backstage to… um… wish Damian luck. I didn't get far though. William Deveaux saw me back there and threatened to report me. I didn't want to cause any trouble, so I just left."

"While you were back there, did you notice anything unusual?" Connie asked. She wasn't sure how reliable Dottie was, but perhaps she saw something.

Just then, a middle-aged couple presented two tickets to Dottie. "Excuse me a moment," she said, then escorted the couple about halfway down a side aisle.

While Dottie sat the couple, Connie and Gianna ribbed their mother.

"We had no idea that you were so into Damian," Gianna said. "Maybe we should warn Dad about your wandering eye."

Jo waved off her daughters. "I was just trying to get her talking about Damian. It's not like you girls could have done it. Damian's more my age, and nobody would believe that one of you had a crush on him."

"I'm impressed," Gianna said. "Maybe Connie gets her detective skills from you."

When Dottie returned, Connie picked up where they left off. "So, did you see anything unusual backstage last night?"

Dottie narrowed her eyes. "Why do you want to know? The police questioned all of us. I don't see how it's any of your business."

Connie remembered from the night before how much of a fan Dottie was of Concetta. "You're right. It's really not my business. But my Aunt Concetta was good friends with Damian, and I can't help but wonder what happened to him."

Dottie appeared to consider Connie's dilemma.

"Look, I'm sorry, but I don't want to talk about it."

Connie tried to press Dottie for more information, but there was no use.

Just as they finished their conversation with Dottie, Grace, Stephanie, and Elyse arrived, and the women took their seats.

"Whatever could you have been discussing with Dottie?" Elyse asked, unable to keep a straight face.

Jo chuckled. "You are one of my daughter's best friends, so I'm guessing you know exactly what Connie was asking her about."

Despite everything, the play was a resounding success. William did a wonderful job as Scrooge, and Stevie gave a first-rate performance as Tiny Tim. Whatever reasons had motivated Eloise to get Stevie involved in acting, one thing was certain: The boy had talent.

After the performance, Elyse, Stephanie, and Grace decided to go home, but Connie managed to convince Jo and Gianna to go to *Surfside Restaurant* for some appetizers and a drink.

"This has become one of my favorite spots," Connie said, after they were seated on the outdoor deck. "Stephanie, Elyse, and I have had many a girls' night out on this very deck."

"I'm so happy that you have made such wonderful friends here in Sapphire Beach," Jo said. "We miss you back home, but it comforts me to know that you are living in my sister's former condo and have such good friends."

"This time last year, moving to Sapphire Beach wasn't even on my radar," Connie said. "It's amazing how quickly life can change."

The women ordered some frozen drinks and nachos and listened to the band playing sixties and seventies music. While the band took a break, the women's conversation drifted toward the events of the past few days.

"I'd be lying if I didn't tell you that, despite my occasional interrogating, I still have mixed feelings about your consistent involvement in these murder investigations," Jo said. "Between your humanitarian work and your Fair Trade business, you've always had this innate sense of justice. It's part of who you are, and I love you for it. But you don't have to jump into every murder case in southwest Florida."

Connie laughed at her mother's dramatic tone. "It's not like I go looking for them. They just seem to find me."

Jo took a sip from her frozen daiquiri. "It's hard for me to argue, because if my sister were still alive, she would be right here with us discussing the investigation. She was never one to sit on the sidelines." Jo's gaze settled on Connie. "The two of you are so much alike in certain ways."

Her mother was right. Connie and Concetta not only shared a name, but they were kindred spirits, even if it wasn't always evident on the surface. Concetta had been a glamorous and wealthy actress, while Connie was more low-key and had been far from wealthy until she inherited her aunt's condo. But they both had the same adventurous spirit. Concetta had left her hometown of Boston for Hollywood after high school to pursue her dream of being an actress, and Connie had left Boston after college to volunteer in Kenya. They had chosen different paths, but both women shared a common passion, generosity, and drive, and they had always loved and supported one another.

This meant that any friend of Concetta's was a friend of Connie's. She had to find out who killed Damian.

Despite her mother's concern, Connie had a feeling that Jo and Gianna would continue to be her trusty sidekicks. It would be fun having them around.

"Let's go over everything we know," Connie said. "There's no danger in doing that."

"At the crime scene, there were two glasses, one with a red lipstick stain, plus an opened bottle of antacid and a candy cane earring," Gianna said, reaching for a nacho. "And you smelled bitter almonds, which indicates cyanide."

"Yes, and Zach also told me he had reason to believe poison was involved," Connie said. "So, I think it's a safe bet that Damian was poisoned."

"Dottie was wearing her candy cane earrings last night, but not tonight," Jo said. "That could be just a coincidence, but it's worth noting."

"And Connie learned from Eloise that Dottie was backstage around the time Damian would have been poisoned," Gianna added.

"It's possible that the earring belonged to a random person who stopped into Damian's dressing room and not the killer," Connie said. "Anyone could have dropped it there."

"Since a lot of people had access to Damian's dressing room," Connie said, "let's try to narrow it down to who had a motive."

"There's Dottie, an obsessed fan who was reprimanded for sneaking backstage," Jo said.

"Dottie said that she considered Damian a good friend, yet, according to Eloise, she annoyed Damian," Gianna said.

"Let's keep her on our short list," Connie said. "Then there's Eloise. When I spoke with Rick this afternoon, he implied that Eloise and Damian had a romantic history."

"Sophie seemed to tense up when Eloise joined our group at the Christmas party," Gianna said.

"I noticed that, too," Jo said.

"Speaking of Sophie," Connie said, "Rick thinks their marriage was in trouble. He said that Damian was planning to move out."

"If that's true, Sophie stood to lose her extravagant lifestyle. That could also be a motive," Gianna said.

"Grace spent some time with her in the theatre last night while the police were questioning people," Jo said. "She said Sophie looked genuinely distraught."

"But don't forget, Mom, Sophie is an actress." Connie sighed and drained the last sip of her frozen mudslide. "From what we know so far, Dottie, Eloise, and Sophie had the strongest motives."

"There's also the question of the Sapphire Beach Playhouse potentially closing," Gianna said.

Connie nodded enthusiastically. "I was thinking that, too. If someone believed Damian was responsible for the theatre potentially closing, or if he was planning to make any unpopular changes, perhaps somebody wanted him out of the picture."

"Speaking of the theatre," Jo said, "did you ever find that key Rick was looking for?"

"I did find two keys that were labeled PH and PH offices. After seeing the key that Rick showed me at the party, I'm guessing one is for the playhouse and the other for the playhouse offices." Connie said. "Thanks for reminding me. With everything that happened, I completely forgot to tell Rick."

Connie's eyes flew wide open as an idea suddenly occurred to her.

"Mom, that's brilliant!" Connie said.

"Wait a minute," Jo said. "I wasn't suggesting…"

But Connie didn't let her finish. "If we can get into the offices, maybe we could see for ourselves how bad the financial problems are or find some type of clue about who Damian's enemies were."

"Since Dad's an accountant," Gianna said, "he'd be the perfect person to take along. He could make quick sense of the financial reports."

Jo shook her head back and forth. "It'll never happen."

Connie motioned for their server to bring the check. "Let's go home and see if we can sweet talk Dad into it."

Chapter 7

"ABSOLUTELY NOT!" Greg said, when his wife and daughters presented their idea to him at 10:30 that night in Connie's living room.

Gary turned off the movie he and Greg had been watching and turned his full attention to the scene unfolding in the living room. "This is better than the movie. We were watching a comedy, but this is way funnier."

"Come on, Dad," Connie said. "It's our best chance to learn who might have had a grudge against Damian."

Greg put both hands on his head. "Let me get this straight. You want me to break into the playhouse offices with you, hack a dead man's computer, and spy on the financials of the Sapphire Beach Playhouse? Are you out of your minds?"

"Well, when you put it that way…" Jo said.

"There's no other way to put it," Greg said.

"The man has a point," Gary chimed. "How would you explain it to your cop boyfriend if you got arrested for breaking and entering?" he asked Connie. "And I'm not comfortable taking the twins to visit their mother in prison. Or their aunt for that matter."

"Thank you, Gary," Greg said.

"Oh my gosh, you two are *so* dramatic," Gianna said, rolling her eyes. "Connie, you were right. I *did* marry Dad."

"Told you," Connie said triumphantly. "I knew that before you even married him. Most of the time that's a good thing – except when Dad's being a scaredy-cat like tonight." Connie batted her eyelashes at her father. "Normally, he's the kindest, most generous, loving man in the whole world."

"No amount of sweet talk is going to persuade me to break into the playhouse offices," Greg said.

"First of all, Dad, we're not breaking in." Connie held up a key. "I have Aunt Concetta's key.

Secondly, we're not going to hack Damian's computer. The police probably already took it to search it. But we do need to know how serious the financial problems were. If Rick was correct, and Damian was about to make some decisions that would affect everyone's career, that could be a motive for murder. The killer might have gotten rid of Damian so that another executive director could be hired, one who might fight harder to save the playhouse. Connie gave him her best Daddy's-little-girl expression. "Please, Dad. It would be a good father-daughter bonding experience."

Connie and Gianna looked at him with pleading eyes.

Connie knew they almost had him, so now was the time to play her last card. "Don't make us do this alone, Dad."

Greg looked to Gary for help, but only found an amused smirk. "How do I let these three women talk me into these things?" he asked.

Connie hugged her father. "Thanks, Dad."

"Yeah, yeah," Greg said, returning her hug. "Just for the record, I think this is a terrible idea. And after an evening with those two little monkeys," he said, pointing toward the bedroom where the twins were sleeping, "all I want to do is turn in. But since I know I won't have any peace unless I go, let's do it now, while it's late and we're less likely to get caught."

"The fewer people who go, the better," Gianna said. "We'll wait here, and you can give us a full report when you return."

Connie changed out of the dress she wore to the play and into more practical clothes, which consisted of navy capri pants, a dark t-shirt, and dark sneakers. She slipped the office key into her pocket and left with her father before he could change his mind.

They parked on a side street so their car wouldn't be seen by passersby and walked around to the front entrance of the small administrative building attached to the theatre. To Connie's delight and Greg's dismay, the key did indeed open the front door.

"Let's get this over with," Greg said.

They entered the office suite, which contained a reception area, a couple of rows of cubicles, and a glass-enclosed office in the back. Connie used the flashlight application on her phone to avoid turning on the lights and attracting unwanted attention. She opened a door on the far right side, next to a long hallway, which she assumed led to the theatre. Behind the door was a room that contained a rectangular mahogany table surrounded by chairs upholstered with blue and gray fabric. She paused for a moment and imagined her aunt, seated at the head of the table, leading board meetings.

The large wall outside the boardroom contained a display of framed photos from various productions throughout the years. Although Concetta had never acted in any of the plays, preferring to stay behind the scenes during her retirement years, there were several photos of Concetta in group shots with various actors.

Connie snapped a closeup of the photos with Concetta, including one of Concetta and Damian posing in front of a giant Christmas tree. Connie guessed that it had been taken at one of Damian's infamous Christmas parties, but their younger-looking faces told her it was from years ago.

"Let's hurry up so we can get out of here," Greg said.

"Okay. I'll start in Damian's office, and you look around out here."

Connie turned on a small desk lamp, since she doubted its light would be visible from the street, and began to search Damian's desk. Unable to find anything interesting, she moved on to the file cabinets, opening each drawer. She found mostly contracts, invoices, and receipts until she finally came to a folder that was labeled "Budgets." Connie grabbed a copy of the last few years' budgets and brought them to her father. "Do these tell you anything?"

After a period of silence that felt like an eternity, Greg confirmed what Connie had hoped wasn't true. "It looks like the Sapphire Beach Playhouse is significantly in the red." He flipped through a few more pages. "It also looks like they have a loan that they are close to defaulting on. According to this, things are pretty bad."

Connie sighed. "So, it's true. The playhouse may have to close. Auntie Concetta would be crushed."

"It looks that way, honey. They behind on their loan payments, and I don't see how they can keep up with that, plus cover their other expenses, with what they are currently bringing in from ticket sales and donations."

Connie snapped a photo of each page of the most recent budget, in case she wanted to refer to it later. "Let's look for a few more minutes to see if we can find anything else."

Connie brought the budgets back to the filing cabinet and placed them back in their file folders. She was about to close the drawer when she noticed another folder entitled "Proposal." There was only one document in the folder, and after scanning its contents, it appeared to be a proposal written by Damian to try to save the playhouse. It included a whole lot of layoffs.

Connie returned to the reception area where her father was anxiously waiting to leave. "Dad, check this out. It looks like Damian was planning to drastically cut staffing."

Greg perused the report. "Wow. He was planning to lay off some of the company's veterans, including many in the artistic department."

"William Deveaux and Rick Bennett are on here," Connie said. "We met them on Thursday night at the Christmas party. I guess the rumors are true. Damian was indeed going to make one last-ditch effort to save the operation, but he was going to do it with only a skeleton crew."

Connie scanned the other names on Damian's termination list but didn't recognize any of them. Noticing a program for "A Christmas Carol" on top of the reception desk, Connie got an idea. She compared the names on the termination list to the cast and crew listed in the program.

"Dad, the only two names on this list of employees to be laid off who are also involved with 'A Christmas Carol' are William and Rick. None of these other people on the list were involved in the play, which means they wouldn't have been backstage when Damian was poisoned."

William and Rick just moved onto Connie's list of suspects.

"We've been in here a long time," Greg said. "We should quit while we're ahead and get out of here."

Connie snapped a picture of the report for future reference, then returned it to where she found it and turned off the desk lamp in Damian's office. Just as they were about to leave, the sound of two approaching voices came from outside the front door.

"Quick, the boardroom," Connie whispered, grabbing her father's arm and pulling him into the adjoining room. Then she pointed to her father's phone. "Turn off your flashlight." She closed the door while he turned off the light emanating from his phone, and they sat on the floor opposite the door, hidden behind by the table. "They'll never find us here," Connie whispered.

"I hope you're right," Greg said. "Nobody will want to hire an accountant with a criminal record."

The front door opened and Rick's voice carried through the office suite. "I could have sworn I saw a light on when we drove by."

Great. Connie would never be able to explain their presence in the boardroom to Rick. And if it did turn out that Rick was the killer, he would know she was investigating. They could *not* get caught.

"What's the big deal about a light being on? The police were in here Friday night searching the offices. They could have left it on. I wouldn't worry about it." Connie recognized the voice as belonging to Rick's wife, Priscilla.

"Well, I don't see a light on," Rick said. "And there are no cars in the parking lot. It must have been my imagination. Still, I think I'll look around just to make sure everything is okay."

The doorknob of the door leading into the board room began to turn. Connie sat breathless and curled up her body as small as she could, as if that would make her less visible.

"Don't bother," Priscilla said. "There's nobody in here. Let's just get out of here. This place is creepy at night."

"Okay, fine," Rick said in a frustrated tone. "Let's go."

Connie let out a quiet sigh of relief and within a couple of minutes, she heard the front door close behind Rick and Priscilla and a car driving away.

"That was close," Connie said.

"The woman was right," Greg said. "This place *is* creepy at night. Let's go."

When they returned home, Jo and Gianna were anxiously waiting up to hear what happened while Gary apparently opted for a good night's sleep. Connie had been half-tempted to call them and say they were in jail as a practical joke, but she decided against it, given that scenario was too close to reality.

"I'm going to bed," Greg said. "Connie can fill you in. But please don't ever ask me to do that again."

Connie kissed her Dad goodnight and thanked him, but she didn't make any promises.

"I have to get to bed," Connie said, after she caught Jo and Gianna up to speed. "It's past midnight, and I have an early morning."

Chapter 8

CONNIE'S ALARM WENT OFF on Sunday morning a minute after her head hit the pillow. Or at least it felt that way. In reality, she probably got about five hours of sleep but it was still a far cry from her preferred eight. She dragged herself out of bed at 6:00 so she could attend the 7:00 Mass and open the shop on time. Her family had opted for a later Mass and were still sleeping when she left.

She arrived at Our Lady, Star of the Sea Church without a minute to spare and quickly scanned the church to find a seat. The size of the congregation was slowly but steadily increasing each week as the chilling temperatures up north pushed the snowbirds down toward warmer weather. She was pleasantly surprised to see Zach amidst the crowd seated a few pews from the back. He usually went to a later Mass since he and Josh normally had weekends off, so Connie figured they must be working overtime on the murder investigation.

When Zach spotted Connie, he smiled warmly and slid further into the pew so Connie could join him.

After Mass, Zach invited Connie for a walk around the beautiful grounds of the church, since they each had some spare time before they were due at work. They strolled across a quaint wooden bridge into a small memorial garden enclosed with lush tropical vegetation and sat next to one another on a granite bench. In the center was a plaque engraved with the names of deceased priests who had served in the parish.

"How's the investigation coming along?" Connie asked

"Unfortunately, by now you know how these things go. There are a lot of people to talk to and leads to follow up on. Josh and I worked all day yesterday to get some of the legwork done. Sergeant Donovan assigned me as the lead investigator, so I'll be at it all day today, as well."

"Have they determined the cause of Damian's death yet?"

Zach's gaze drifted toward the blue skies beyond the garden, then back at Connie. "It looks like your guess was on target. We discovered a lethal dose of cyanide in Damian's bottle of antacid," Zach said. "Damian and his family were in my prayers all during Mass."

Connie let out a deep breath. "So, he was definitely murdered." Even though it looked unlikely, Connie had still been holding on to a shred of hope that Damian's death had been the result of a natural cause. But now she knew that somebody had actually killed her aunt's friend, and the killer could have been someone that Concetta knew. Tears stung at the back of Connie's eyes. She had come face to face with murder in the past, but it never got easier.

"Are you okay?" Zach asked.

Connie nodded. "It's just such a waste. The killer obviously knew Damian well enough to know his pre-performance routine. And that person thought that there was no other solution to whatever problem he or she had with Damian than to take his life."

"It seems that way. We are looking at everyone who had backstage access at any point that night."

Connie thought of Dottie and was wondering if she should mention what she learned. But she didn't have to wonder for long. Zach seemed to read her thoughts.

"What is it?" he asked. "Did you remember something?"

"It may not be important, but I met an usher named Dottie McKenzie on Friday night, when the play was supposed to open. She was wearing my candy cane earrings, but the following night, when we went back to see the play, she wasn't wearing them. It could be nothing, but when I asked her about it, she got all uncomfortable. And from what I hear, it wasn't unusual for her to go backstage to try to talk to Damian. There were even complaints against her."

"I knew she was backstage, but thanks for letting me know about the earrings. Dottie is on my list of people to follow up with." Then he flashed her a playful smile. "But I didn't invite you for a walk to talk about the case, you know."

"I guess you probably didn't. Did you have any particular topic in mind, or shall I choose one at random?" she asked, teasing him. She had the feeling it was the former.

"I'd rather talk about that second date that hasn't happened yet."

"That sounds like an interesting topic."

"I know it's a busy season, especially with your family being in town and your fundraiser, but it seems like we're both always busy with something. I was hoping you might be able to find some time for that date in the next couple of weeks."

So, this second date was really going to happen. And soon. Connie couldn't have been happier. "I think I can find an evening to break away. Grace and Abby have both turned out to be very capable employees, so I've finally been able to take some time off."

"Would next Sunday night work? I've been wanting to check out the snow in Naples."

Connie gave him a puzzled look. "The snow?"

Zach laughed. "Artificial snow. Every evening on Third Street South this time of year they pipe in artificial snow and the street becomes like a winter wonderland. It's a little touristy, but I hear it's fun. We could grab dinner nearby and then check it out."

"That sounds great," Connie said. "It will be nice to slow down for a few hours and enjoy the season."

After Zach walked Connie back to her car, she made a quick stop home to pick up Ginger - partly to give the dog another respite from her exuberant playmates, but also because Connie missed her favorite chestnut-and-white-furred sidekick. Then she headed to the shop.

Sunday morning was Connie's favorite time downtown. Peace and quiet rested upon the streets since many people were at church or home enjoying a leisurely morning. She had just enough time for a stroll with Ginger through the downtown streets before opening the store and getting to work on more candy cane earrings.

As usual, Grace attended the 9:00 Mass and arrived like clockwork at little after 10:00, with two coffees in hand.

Connie's eyes grew wide when Grace handed her one of the steaming cups. "Perfect timing. I had a late night and could use a jolt of caffeine."

"I heard. Your father filled me in on your adventure last night. I wish I could have been a fly on the wall," Grace said, laughing.

Grace's laughter was contagious. "Let's just say it was a father-daughter adventure I'll never forget."

After a slow but steady morning, business started to pick up. Connie was surprised when she saw William Deveaux among her customers, with a woman whom Connie assumed to be his wife.

"Is this Connie?" the woman asked, marching over to where Connie stood and shaking her hand. "I'm Judith, William's wife." She moved a strand of dark brown hair so that Connie could see she was wearing candy cane earrings. "I just love these earrings and am so inspired by the fundraiser you are doing for such a worthy cause."

"We came for a stroll downtown, and when we spotted your shop, we just had to drop by," William said. "My wife wanted to see your Fair Trade jewelry."

Connie led Judith over to the Fair Trade section, then left her to shop.

"I'm sorry for your loss," Connie said, rejoining William by the table, while Judith perused the jewelry.

He gave her a puzzled look.

"Damian?" Connie said. Could he really be that dense?

"Oh, yes, yes," he said, changing his expression to appear sorrowful. "Poor Damian."

It didn't appear as though William was laboring under any grief. She wondered if his carelessness was related to Damian's proposal to lay him off.

"The police are treating it as a homicide, since there were suspicious circumstances surrounding his death," Connie said, probing for a reaction. "Being the executive director of the playhouse, Damian must have had some enemies. It's never easy making tough decisions."

"I certainly hope nothing shady like that happened at our little theatre," he said. "It's true that not everyone agreed with Damian's vision for the future of the playhouse, but it's hard to imagine that anyone would kill him over it."

So, he did know something about Damian's plan.

"Someone clearly didn't want him around," Connie said. "You must have spent a lot of time with him over the years, William. Do you have any idea who could have wanted to harm him?"

"You know, anything I could tell you would only be my own opinion, and I hate to gossip..." His voice rose and octave toward the end of the sentence.

As soon as William said the word "gossip," Judith turned around. She put down the jewelry she was browsing and came over to join Connie and William.

"Yes, we hate to gossip," she said, nodding solemnly. "What are we gossiping about?"

"Damian, dear. Connie was just asking if we knew who might want to harm him."

"Oh, yes, Damian." Judith shook her head back and forth. "We are just beside ourselves."

"Well," William said, "it's hard to know what could drive someone to kill another person, but I can tell you that Rick is carrying a mountain of debt. He told me that if he got laid off, he would probably have to declare bankruptcy. That's why I am considering a job offer I received from a playhouse in Sarasota. Quite honestly, the writing has been on the wall for some time now, so I've been putting out feelers. Besides, I'm not getting the parts that I'd like to be getting here in Sapphire Beach."

If William had another job option, that would make it a lot less likely that he'd kill Damian to keep his job.

"But that's nothing," Judith said. "Did you tell Connie about Eloise?"

"No, dear, I haven't gotten to that yet."

"I understand that Damian and Eloise were old friends and acted together years ago," Connie said. She also knew they were involved but wanted to hear what William knew.

"That's true," William said. "But there's a lot more to it." He looked around the store, but not seeing anyone within earshot, he leaned closer to Connie. "They had a pretty steamy relationship back in the day - a relationship that they picked back up about eight years ago."

Connie studied their expressions. Clearly, she was supposed to put something together based on what he said. She took a stab at it. "How long ago did Eloise marry Stephen?"

"Ten years ago."

"Oh, I see. So, they were having an affair." Connie reflected for a moment.

"Did Eloise want Damian to leave his wife?"

William shook his head. "No. She regretted the affair and wanted to make things work with Stephen."

"So why would she kill Damian?"

Then it hit Connie, and her jaw nearly fell to the ground.

"Wait a minute! Stevie is seven years old. Are you saying that Stevie is Damian's son?"

Well, that certainly opened up some new possibilities. Maybe Sophie found out. Or, if Damian had threatened to expose their secret, perhaps Eloise killed him. Connie remembered that Stephen had been out of town all week and wasn't in the theatre the night Damian was killed, so it couldn't have been him.

"How many people know this?"

"It's hard to keep a secret in the theatre world. I'd say pretty much everyone except Stevie, Stephen, and Sophie." William let out a devious chuckle. "Damian was furious that Eloise named him Stevie, after her husband. But there was nothing he could do, because he didn't want Sophie finding out about the affair."

"But rumor had it," Judith said, "that Damian was preparing to leave Sophie anyway and wanted Eloise to tell Stephen the truth. And he wanted Stevie to know he was his father."

"That would have been traumatic for poor Stevie," Connie said. "I can see why Eloise would have been against it. Not to mention that it would likely have meant the end of her marriage." Connie thought for a moment. "How determined was Damian to tell Stevie?"

"Damian and Eloise were seen several times in a heated discussion," William said. "So, I'm guessing it was becoming an issue."

"Who knows how far Eloise would go to protect her marriage and the well-being of her little boy," Judith said. "If you ask me, Eloise had the most to gain by his death."

She did make a valid point.

Chapter 9

AS SUNDAY AFTERNOON wore on, the downtown streets of Sapphire Beach swelled with holiday shoppers. With only nine shopping days until Christmas Eve, people seemed to be taking advantage of the sunny 76-degree day to wander in and out of shops. And since Connie's jewelry could easily fit into a suitcase, it made a great gift for people who were travelling for the holidays.

The candy cane earrings were selling well, too. The window display that Connie created was drawing customers in to ask about the fundraiser. In addition to purchasing a pair of earrings, they often also chose to buy Fair Trade pieces in the spirit of the holidays. Connie always included a biography of the artisan for the recipient of the gift and asked her customers to spread the word to friends - a request that was usually received with enthusiasm.

Connie had to smile as it occurred to her that the fundraiser was increasing business. The old adage, "In giving we receive" seemed to be holding true. Although it hadn't been Connie's intent, due to the extra traffic because of the fundraiser, Connie would likely make back all the money she had personally invested in supplies for the candy cane earrings. However, there was still a lot of work ahead and no guarantee that they would be able to meet their goal of $4,000 in the next nine days.

Just as Grace was about to leave for the afternoon, several students from Connie's Thursday evening jewelry-making class surprised her by coming to make earrings. Elyse brought Emma, who was becoming quite the jewelry maker, and her Great Aunt Gertrude. Ruby, the owner of the souvenir shop next door, had coverage in her own store, so she came, as well. And Abby arrived early for her shift so she could bang out some extra pairs of earrings.

"You ladies are a sight for sore eyes," Connie said. "I was beginning to worry that we'd never finish the earrings."

"Abby texted us to let us know there were still a lot more left to be made if we are to meet our goal, so here we are," Ruby said. She pointed to a pink and white pastry box that Abby was carrying. "And she even brought cookies."

Connie was thrilled that everyone was rallying around the fundraising project. "Remind me to make you Employee of the Month," she said to Abby.

"What about Grace?"

"How about you each get the honor every other month?"

Abby chuckled. "Works for me."

Grace winked at Abby. "Me, too. Now that all the fun is about to begin, I'm staying."

While everyone settled into an earring-making rhythm, Connie and Grace brought out some pitchers of lemonade for the women to enjoy with their cookies. Connie joined them as much as she could, in between waiting on customers. She also snapped a few photos of the women working, as well as some close-ups of the finished products to upload to her social media outlets to draw in customers. It would take a load off Connie's mind to have the earrings completed so she could focus all her effort on selling them.

As Connie uploaded the photos, she listened to the women catch up on one another's lives. Although they varied in age – from now twelve-year-old Emma to Gertrude, who was in her eighties, their love for jewelry making and their generous hearts brought them together this afternoon to volunteer their free time.

"How's your senior year going, Abby?" Elyse asked. Although Elyse mainly came to bring Emma and Gertrude, the earrings were relatively simple to make, so she was working at the table with the others.

"I'm enjoying the year with my friends, but I can't wait until grad school next year. I applied for early admission to Florida Sands University's doctoral program in American Literature, so, as long as I get in, I'll be living in the area for the foreseeable future."

It had been Abby's dream since she was a teenager to be a professor and writer, so Connie was happy to see her one step closer to making her dream a reality.

"That's wonderful," Ruby said. "I expect a signed copy of your first book."

"You got it."

By the time the women were ready to leave, Connie had another fifty pairs to add to the basket. After doing a quick count of sales and remaining inventory, Connie announced that they only had forty more to go. Abby had promised to continue to work diligently in between customers until the shop closed that evening, and the others promised to return on Thursday evening to finish up if necessary.

When everyone left, Connie decided to leave the store in Abby's capable hands and take a rare Sunday evening off. Connie fastened a leash on Ginger, and as she and Grace walked toward their cars together, Connie caught Grace up to speed on her investigating.

"Even though a lot of people had backstage access, I managed to narrow down a list of suspects based on people who were both backstage on Friday night, and who also had a motive. But I wish I knew more about some of these people."

"It sounds like you need additional insight from someone who knows all the people involved." Grace narrowed her eyes and rubbed her chin. "I think I know somebody who can help you. Can you spare some time right now?"

"Absolutely," Connie said.

"I'll follow you back to Palm Paradise, and by the time we get there, I should know if my idea will pan out."

It was only a few minutes' drive back to Palm Paradise. When they arrived, they parked their cars in their assigned spots in the underground garage, and as Connie exited her car, Grace motioned for her to get into her own car.

"What's going on?" Connie asked.

"I just got off the phone with a dear old friend of Concetta's and mine, Peter Holloway. He is on the Board of Directors for the Sapphire Beach Playhouse and I told him about you – not the investigation, just that you lived in Concetta's condo and that your family was in town for the play. He said he would love to meet you."

Connie squeezed Grace's forearm. "Great thinking. Maybe he can give us some information that will lead us to the killer."

"That's what I was thinking. Come on," Grace said. "I also called your mother, and she and your sister are coming with us. We're picking them up at the front entrance."

"You're the best. The more of us who come, the less suspicious we will look. Besides, we'd never hear the end of it if we left them out."

While they were driving, Connie caught the women up on her conversation with Zach that morning after Mass. She should have expected it, but Connie was still surprised when she got more of a reaction from her news that she had a second date with Zach than about Damian's antacid containing cyanide.

Twenty minutes later, Connie, Grace, Jo, and Gianna were seated in Mr. Peter Holloway's living room, enjoying tea and macaroons. He was a gracious man with white hair and green eyes who appeared to be in his eighties. Connie guessed he had been quite handsome in his day.

"How lovely of you to pay me a visit," he said. "My late wife, Carol, and I were big fans of Concetta's. We both served on the Board of Directors with her for, goodness, I'd say seven years.

I was so happy to hear that Damian and the cast decided to dedicate this season's production in her memory. She did so much for the playhouse during her tenure."

"My sister would have been thrilled, Mr. Holloway," Jo said. "The playhouse meant the world to her."

"Please, you can all call me Peter." A distant expression spread across his face. "Yes, things haven't been going so well the past couple of years."

"That's what we heard," Gianna said. "Apparently the playhouse is having some financial difficulties."

"It would be a shame if it had to close," Grace said. "The performances provide so much culture and entertainment to the Sapphire Beach community."

"Unfortunately, the rumors *are* true," Peter said. "I resigned from the board six months ago. I let everyone think it was because I was getting too old and tired to continue, but the truth is, I didn't like the direction things were heading. And I don't just mean financially. I witnessed too much backstabbing among the staff in the last couple of years, and it made me uncomfortable. Hearing about what happened to Damian confirmed that I made the right choice. I hear that his death is now officially a murder investigation."

Grace nodded. "That's what we heard, too."

"We attended Damian's annual Christmas party on Thursday night," Connie said. "It seemed like Damian was a well-loved member of the community. It's hard to imagine that anyone would wish to harm him."

Peter looked away.

"Is there something you know, Peter?" Grace asked. "You can trust these folks. Connie has helped solve a few murder investigations since she's moved to Sapphire Beach."

"My aunt was fond of Damian and of the playhouse," Connie said. "We just want to see justice served."

Peter looked at Grace, then back at Connie. "I hate to say it, but if I were the police, I would look into Rick Bennett."

"The director of the play?" Jo asked. "Why would you say that?"

"Well, it's no secret that Damian had to either make some serious cutbacks, including staffing, or risk going bankrupt, but Rick was convinced that he had a better plan to save it. In fact, Rick competed with Damian for the position of executive director years back but lost out by a slim margin. The Board was in a deadlock for weeks deciding who to hire. I happen to know that Rick recently took several board members to dinner and proposed a plan for raising the needed funds. He had some good ideas, too."

"But that would have meant firing Damian," Gianna said.

"Yes, and the Board wasn't likely to do that. Rick had convinced a few members, but not nearly a majority."

"Do you think he wanted the job badly enough to kill for it?" Connie asked.

"I don't know. I've been asking myself the same question ever since I heard about Damian's suspicious death. But one thing is for sure. Rick was actively campaigning for Damian's job."

Chapter 10

THE WOMEN WALKED to the car in silence after their conversation with Peter Holloway.

"I guess we can move Rick Bennett up a few notches on our list of suspects," Connie finally said, as Grace backed out of Peter's driveway.

"When I would go to social events for the playhouse with Concetta, I never realized there was so much going on beneath the surface," Grace said. "Ignorance really is bliss."

"It certainly is an interesting cast of characters. Pun intended," Connie said with a smirk.

When they got home, nobody felt like cooking, so they ordered pizza for dinner. Jo and Gianna had told the guys that they were out running some errands, so they didn't ask any questions when they returned.

Connie had the feeling that they suspected the women were up to something but chose not to ask.

Grace joined them for pizza, but as soon as they finished eating, she headed home for a quiet evening alone. After Gary and Gianna put the twins to bed, the guys announced that they wanted to catch the rest of the football game on TV, so the women opted for a glass of wine on the balcony.

Jo closed the slider behind them for privacy. "So, what did you girls think of our visit with Peter?"

"It definitely gives Rick a strong motive," Gianna said. "And as the director, he would have known Damian's pre-performance routine and had easy access to Damian's dressing room."

"I'd say Rick is a strong suspect," Jo said.

"William Deveaux and his wife, Judith, came into my store this morning," Connie said. "They mentioned that Rick was on the verge of declaring bankruptcy and losing everything. William also revealed that he had a job offer from another theatre, so I don't think he'd kill Damian over a job he didn't need."

"Rick is a strong suspect, but I still haven't crossed Dottie off my list," Gianna said.

Jo shook her head. "Me, neither. I don't like that she was sneaking around backstage. She could have easily slipped into Damian's dressing room and poisoned his antacid."

"And if she was as obsessed with him as everybody says, she likely knew his routine," Connie added. "But don't forget, there's still Eloise and Sophie to consider. Eloise and Damian were seen in a heated argument several times recently, and Sophie stood to lose a lot financially if Damian left her, which Dottie and Rick both thought he was considering doing. Eloise and Sophie both had motives and backstage access."

Connie drained her last sip of wine, and fatigue suddenly overtook her. "The only thing I know for sure is that I'm too tired to think straight anymore. After my late adventure with Dad last night and a long day today, I need to go to bed."

"You get a good night's sleep, sweetie, so you can enjoy the boat ride tomorrow."

Betty, an old acquaintance of Concetta's, owned a pontoon boat that she kept in a marina in Naples and offered rides for a small fee in order to earn extra income. It was an informal service only available to friends via word of mouth, but since Connie and her family had done it in the past, Jo called Betty and arranged a tour. Grace agreed to work a little later than she normally did on Mondays, so Connie could enjoy the excursion with her family.

The following morning, Connie was the last one up. She must have been more tired than she thought, because she slept a full ten hours before finally getting out of bed at 8:00. Thankfully, her sister had kept the twins out of her room so she could sleep, and that couldn't have been an easy task.

After opening her eyes to the smell of bacon wafting through the condo, Connie hopped in the shower, then groggily made her way to the kitchen, where a plate of eggs, potatoes, bacon, and fruit was waiting for her on the counter and a pot of coffee had just finished brewing.

Ginger stayed close by Connie's side while she took her plate to the dining room table, and her mother kept her company while she ate. She slipped the dog a small piece of bacon.

"Your father and I took Ginger for a long walk earlier so you could take it easy and enjoy the morning."

She said a silent prayer of thanksgiving for the meal, then smiled gratefully at her mother. "Thanks, Mom. I feel like a new woman after sleeping for so long. And I can't wait to dig into this breakfast."

Jo smiled. "Enjoy."

Within an hour, the Petretta/Bianchi clan had loaded themselves into two cars and were driving down Route 75 South into Naples, where they were greeted by Betty, their captain.

"Is this your first time on a boat?" she asked, bending down to speak with the twins, who were practically jumping with excitement as they nodded that it was.

"Well, the first thing we do is put on our life vests." Betty had vests of all sizes, and as soon as everyone was fitted, they boarded the small vessel.

There were two seats in the bow of the boat and a u-shape padded bench in the stern. The sun shone strongly in the bright blue sky, and the temperature had climbed into the low eighties.

"You chose the perfect day," Betty said as they settled into their seats.

In no time, they were cruising across the crystal waters of the Gulf of Mexico.

"There's nothing like the feel of the wind through your hair on a beautiful day," Gianna said.

Connie's favorite part was watching the experience through Hannah and Noah's eyes. The twins entertained the family, chatting up the seagulls that flew a short distance away. When two dolphins followed behind the boat, they squealed with joy, as if the dolphins were personally welcoming them into their exclusive playground. Between the entertainment provided by the twins, the spray of saltwater against her warm skin and the company of loved ones, Connie couldn't ask for more. She hadn't realized how much she needed this distraction.

After a couple of hours of playing on the water, Betty took them back to the marina.

Greg and Jo offered to take the family out to lunch, so they stopped at a restaurant in an outdoor shopping mall on the way home, where they opted for a shaded outdoor table. The patio was decorated with white Christmas lights and featured a tall, thin Christmas tree in the corner with a Santa display next to the tree.

"I'll never get used to looking at Christmas decorations while sitting outdoors in shorts and a t-shirt," Greg said.

"It's heaven on earth, if you ask me," Jo said.

They enjoyed a leisurely lunch while people-watching and talking about past Christmases.

As Connie finished her turkey club sandwich, Dottie and a friend walked onto the patio and were seated a few tables away.

Connie went over to say hello while Greg paid for lunch. "Hi, Dottie," Connie said. "I saw you come in and just wanted to say hello. It's a perfect day to eat outdoors."

"Hi Connie," Dottie said. "Yes, it's a lovely day."

"How has the play been doing?"

Dottie looked away with a scowl. It was as if the play was the last thing she wanted to talk about.

"The play seems to be doing well. Yesterday's performances were sold out, and I hear it's the same for tomorrow's. I'm taking a little break today, since the theatre is closed on Mondays."

"I'm glad to hear it's going well, especially with everything that happened on Friday. I've been thinking about it a lot, and…"

Connie couldn't get out the rest of the sentence before Dottie cut her off. "Look, Connie, I know the playhouse was special to your aunt, but I think you should stay away from the investigation." Dottie looked squarely at Connie. "You shouldn't meddle where you don't belong, or you might get hurt."

Connie was taken aback. Was this a threat or genuine concern?

"Well, I'll let you get back to your family. It was nice seeing you," Dottie said, returning her attention to the menu she was holding.

Talk about getting brushed off. Dottie usually had a pleasant disposition, at least from what Connie had seen of it at the theatre.

Connie smiled politely at Dottie, then at Dottie's friend. "Well, I won't keep you. Enjoy your meal." Then she rejoined her family, who was ready to leave.

"That was strange," Connie said when they were a safe distance away. "Dottie clearly didn't want to talk to me. She completely brushed me off."

"I wouldn't take it personally. She was probably just preoccupied," Gianna said.

"Maybe." But Connie had the feeling there was more to it.

As soon as they returned to Palm Paradise, Connie headed straight to work and made it to *Just Jewelry* by 2:00.

The rest of Monday, as well as Tuesday and Wednesday, seemed to fly by. Business was picking up as the number of shopping days dwindled, and Connie's family was spending most of their time relaxing in the sun and playing with the twins on the beach or at the pool. Abby kindly worked a few unscheduled hours on Tuesday morning so Connie, her family, and Grace could all attend Damian's funeral.

On Thursday morning, a few minutes after Connie opened the store, William and Judith Deveaux came bounding into the shop. They looked as though they were bursting at the seams with something to say.

They headed straight to Connie, who was sitting at table working on the last of the candy cane earrings, which she hoped to finish that night with the help of her class.

Connie stood to greet them. "Welcome back to *Just Jewelry*. It's nice to see you again."

Judith didn't waste any time with small talk. "Did you hear that Dottie McKenzie went missing?"

"What do you mean *missing*?" Connie asked. "I just saw her on Monday."

William and Judith sat across from Connie. "She disappeared halfway through her shift at last night's performance and never returned," William said. "Kathy, the volunteer coordinator in charge of scheduling the ushers, tried repeatedly to reach her by phone but was unsuccessful. Nobody has been able to find her anywhere. It's as if she just vanished from the theatre."

Connie remembered how Dottie had been acting strangely when she ran into her on Monday, even urging Connie to stay away from the case. Had she felt unsafe?

"Do you know who saw her last?" Connie asked

"According to one of the other ushers, Maxine, Dottie was standing at the back of the theatre watching the show just after intermission," William said. "Then, the next time she looked, Dottie was gone." His eyes widened. "I'll bet her disappearance is connected with Damian's murder."

"Or maybe she was kidnapped because she knows who the killer is," Judith said, expressing more intrigue at the mystery than concern over Dottie's well-being.

"I doubt she would have been kidnapped in the middle of the play," Connie said. "But maybe something happened to cause her to run away." Connie was losing her patience with their cavalier attitude, but she hid her annoyance, since she didn't want to discourage them from bringing her information in the future.

"We can't stay long," William said. "We just wanted to be sure you heard the news." And they left the shop as quickly as they came.

Connie would definitely have to speak with Maxine and hear firsthand what happened last night. But the interview would have to wait, since she would be alone in the store all day and meeting with her jewelry making class that evening. The soonest she would be able to get to the theatre would be the following evening when Abby would be working.

Connie's all-star jewelry-making class did not disappoint. Her students showed up early and worked diligently on finishing the last of the candy cane earrings. By the end of the night, Connie was able to breathe a sigh of relief as all two hundred pairs were complete, plus a few extra for good measure.

The class didn't stop at just creating the earrings. Many of them came with orders and checks from pairs they had sold. Between what Damian had purchased for the cast, the orders her students had brought, and the earrings that had been sold in the store, they were more than halfway toward meeting their goal. It would be cutting it close, but their chicken coop had a solid chance of coming to fruition.

When class ended, it was 9:00 and time to close up shop. Connie straightened up and headed back to Palm Paradise.

She joined her family on the balcony, and eventually the conversation turned toward the investigation.

"Have you broken into any more buildings without me?" Greg asked his daughter.

"Of course not," Connie said. "You know I save all my breaking and entering for quality time with my dad."

After Connie filled everyone in on Dottie's disappearance, Jo, Greg, and Gary retired for the evening, leaving Connie alone with Gianna.

Gianna gave her sister a devious look. "Now that they're gone, what's our next step?"

Connie had to smile. Her sister knew her well. "I'm going to stop by Sophie's in the morning, since she's the one person we haven't been able to speak with yet, and also go by the theatre before tomorrow night's performance to see if I can catch Maxine. Maybe she saw something the evening Dottie disappeared."

Connie hadn't wanted to be disrespectful by visiting Sophie while she was in mourning, but now that the funeral was over, she felt better about it.

"What time are we leaving for Sophie's?"

Connie laughed. "Grace is working in the morning, so I can cut out any time. How about I pick you up here at 11:00?"

"Perfect," Gi said. "I'll make a casserole, so we have a good excuse to stop by."

"We'd better tell Mom. She'll be crushed if we don't include her."

Chapter 11

CONNIE PICKED UP GIANNA and Jo right on schedule at 11:00 on Friday morning, and they drove to the palatial home of Damian's widow, Sophie Michel-Pritchard.

Connie's stomach sank as they made their way down the long walkway leading to the front door of the Pritchard home.

"It's hard to believe we were here just over a week ago under such different circumstances," Connie said. Last Thursday, she had been so excited for the party and for the opening of the play the following night. "I found Sophie's phone number in Auntie Concetta's address book, so I called her to let her know we were stopping by."

Gianna rang the doorbell, and within a few seconds Sophie greeted them from the other side of the doorway. Her hair and makeup were flawless, and she was dressed to the nines. She reminded Connie more of how a character on TV would appear when receiving guests on a weekday morning than a real person.

"You don't mind if we sit on the lanai, do you?" Sophie asked. "The house is an absolute mess."

Connie recalled all the servants that were working at the party last week and wondered how the house could possibly be a mess, but perhaps Sophie had unusually high standards.

"Of course not," Jo said graciously. "We should take advantage of the beautiful morning."

Gianna handed the chicken casserole she had made to Sophie, who received it with a half-smile.

"That's very sweet of you ladies. It reminds me of something Concetta would have done. She would have made something, too, rather than buy it, as most of my friends tend to do." Then she shook her head, as if reprimanding herself. "Don't mind me. I don't mean to sound ungrateful. It's just the personal touch means so much during a difficult time like this."

"Of course," Gianna said. "No need to explain. We hope you enjoy it."

Sophie walked them to a seating area on the lanai, then went inside to get some iced tea and put the casserole in the refrigerator.

"We are so sorry for your loss," Jo said, when she returned. "How are you doing?"

"As well as can be expected, I suppose. I still don't think it's hit me yet that Damian is really gone."

"Be patient with yourself. It takes time," Jo said.

"It was such a shock. It's not like he was sick and I had time to come to terms with losing him. Someone just up and killed him," Sophie said with a shaky voice.

"I can't imagine what you must be going through," Gianna said.

"Damian was very kind to us, inviting us to your home and to opening night, and purchasing earrings to benefit the fundraiser," Connie said.

Jo nodded in agreement. "Not to mention that any friend of Concetta's is a friend of ours."

"Since Friday night, we've been trying to figure out who could have done this to him," Connie said.

"Did Damian have any enemies that you know of?" Connie studied Sophie's reactions, but actors were hard to read. Connie wanted to be sympathetic, in case her grief was sincere, but she didn't want to take her at face value, either. After all, she could be talking with a killer.

Sophie remained silent for a moment. "Doesn't everybody have enemies? Concetta was such a wonderful fundraiser because of her popularity and hard work, but once she passed away, donations plummeted. It wasn't Damian's fault. In fact, he was the one who got Concetta to join the Board of Directors in the first place. But everyone seemed to blame him, anyway. Some people, like Rick Bennett, thought they could do a better job running the playhouse." Sophie shook her head. "Damian knew he was vying for his job. And then there's William. He and Judith are huge gossips and much too wrapped up in appearances. William would be devastated if he were to be laid off. But for either of them to kill Damian over these things? I don't know."

"William told me that he received another job offer that he is considering," Connie said.

136

"I'm glad to hear that," Sophie said. "It's probably for the best."

"You're right about one thing," Connie said. "People certainly are passionate about the playhouse. Many people seem to depend on its success for their livelihood and their status in the community."

"It would be a tremendous loss if it had to close," Gianna added.

"Besides those who didn't agree with Damian's business plan, can you think of anyone else? Did he have any obsessive fans that might have been off kilter?" Connie asked. She was curious to see if Sophie would bring up Dottie.

"You mean Dottie McKenzie?" Sophie asked.

"Her name has come up a few times."

"William and Judith stopped by yesterday and told me she went missing. I can't help but wonder if she ran away because she's guilty," Sophie said. "She was always trying to sneak a visit with Damian backstage. She carried a huge torch for him. He tried to be polite, but it was getting out of hand. Damian spoke to Rick about it, and if she was caught one more time, she was going to be fired."

"Dottie is certainly a possibility," Connie said. "Can you think of anyone else?"

Sophie narrowed her eyes.

"What is it?" Jo asked.

"I saw Eloise and Damian fighting on a couple of occasions. I'm no fool. I saw the way she used to look at my husband, and I know they were in a relationship back when they lived in California. Maybe she wanted Damian to leave me and he refused, so she got angry and killed him."

"You think Eloise was willing to leave Stevie's father for Damian?" Connie asked, studying Sophie for any indication that she knew about Damian and Eloise's more recent affair or that Damian was Stevie's father.

Sophie shrugged, then looked directly into Connie's eyes. "All I know is that Damian and I were happily married. Why else would she have been so angry at him if she didn't have feelings for him? In my experience, where there's passion, there's either intense love or hate, and Eloise had no reason to hate Damian."

Since Sophie didn't even flinch when Connie mentioned Stevie, Connie doubted that Sophie knew

Damian was Stevie's biological father. But she couldn't be certain. Also, she stated with unwavering confidence that she and Damian were happily married. If that were true, and Damian was not planning to leave her, she would have no financial motive to kill him, either. She would be better off financially with Damian alive. However, Sophie *was* an actress. Maybe Connie had just witnessed a convincing performance.

They chatted for a while longer, then, after assuring Sophie that they would keep her in their prayers, Connie, Jo, and Gianna left.

"Since our tree-decorating party is tonight, why don't we stop and get the Christmas tree now?" Connie suggested.

"Great idea," Gianna said, "That way you don't have to leave work too early tonight."

It was a longstanding tradition in the Petretta family to wait until the weekend before Christmas to decorate the tree, so although Connie's condo had looked like a Christmas wonderland since the day after Thanksgiving, she patiently waited for the appointed weekend to put up the tree. Connie had invited Grace, the Millers, Zach, and Stephanie to join her family in the festivities later that night, and she was thrilled that everyone could make it.

"It was a wonderful idea to have everyone over tonight," Jo said. "That way we will all have the chance to get better acquainted before Christmas Day."

That's what Connie was hoping.

"I'm still not convinced that I'm going to like having an artificial tree," Connie said, as they pulled into the parking lot.

"Just give it a chance," Jo said. "I think it will work better in this climate."

"Are you sure Auntie Concetta didn't own a Christmas tree?" Gianna asked. "Did you check the storage bin?"

"I'm positive," Connie said. "I gave away a lot of her things to the parish thrift shop when I moved in to make room for my stuff, and there was definitely no tree. She did have a few decorations, which I kept."

"I'm not surprised," Jo said. "My sister usually spent Christmas with us in Massachusetts, so why would she have a tree?"

Being the home decorating experts in the family, Jo and Gianna took over the tree-selecting decisions and chose a blue spruce with snow-kissed branches and white lights, which, Connie had to admit, would look beautiful in the corner of the living room, in front of the double slider windows.

They also purchased a deep red tree skirt with a white fur-lined border and some gold garland. Since Connie had brought her ornaments when she moved, they were all set on that front.

"How are we going to fit everyone into the apartment tonight?" Connie asked as they were driving home, with the boxed tree precariously loaded into the trunk. They had been assisted by an overenthusiastic teenager, who they later learned was on his first day on the job. Fortunately, it would be a quick drive home.

"Don't worry about that, honey. When your father and I first got married, there were many occasions when we crammed both our families into a tiny one bedroom apartment. Besides, it will be a good trial run for Christmas Day."

When they arrived back at Palm Paradise, the guys came downstairs to lug up the tree. Connie went upstairs to make herself a quick sandwich, then arrived back at *Just Jewelry* in time to relieve Grace for the busiest part of the day. Connie was pleased to see that there were several customers browsing and a short line at the checkout counter.

Business remained steady until 4:00, when Abby arrived.

Connie worked with Abby until things slowed down around dinnertime. During the lull in activity, she glanced at her phone to check the time. If she left now, she would have just enough time to catch Maxine at the playhouse before things got too busy and still make it home in time for her company.

Chapter 12

CONNIE SPOTTED MAXINE milling around the theatre, apparently waiting for patrons to arrive, and casually struck up a conversation.

"Hi Maxine, I'm Connie. We met briefly on opening night," she said, trying to jog the usher's memory. "I was talking with Dottie."

"Oh. Hi, Connie," Maxine said. "It's nice to see you again."

Connie could tell by Maxine's blank expression that she was just pretending to remember her so as not to offend her. Connie couldn't help but smile at the woman's politeness.

"Any friend of Dottie's is a friend of mine," Maxine said.

Connie didn't correct Maxine's assumption that she and Dottie were friends. And she definitely wasn't going to mention that Dottie had told her to stay out of the investigation.

"I'm concerned about Dottie. I heard that she is missing and was wondering if you saw anything unusual the night she disappeared."

Maxine's eyes grew moist, and she shook her head. "No. I just can't understand what happened. Everything seemed completely normal up until the time she vanished. Maybe if I had been more aware, she would be here with me tonight."

Connie's heart went out to the woman. Although it wasn't Maxine's fault, Connie could understand how she might feel as if she could have done something, since she was the last person to see Dottie. "Maxine, I'm sure it was a busy night, and the theatre was dark. Please don't blame yourself."

"I know," Maxine said. "I just wish I saw something helpful."

"Maybe you did," Connie said. "You said things seemed normal *up until* she vanished? What happened just before she disappeared?"

Maxine pulled a tissue from the pocket of her green blazer and dabbed her eyes. "We were talking to patrons and having a good time, like we usually did when we worked together. The next thing I knew, she was reading a note, and she looked upset. I asked her what was wrong, but she brushed me off. I left to seat a couple, and when I returned, she was gone."

"Has Dottie ever left in the middle of a shift before?"

"No, never. She could be a little silly about the actors, especially Damian Pritchard. It's no secret that she had a major crush on him. Sometimes she would slip backstage before the patrons began arriving, hoping to run into him. But she was a responsible usher. She wouldn't have left her post without a reason. You must know that since you are friends."

"Of course," Connie said. "I just wanted to see if you saw anything unusual since you were here. I ran into her on Monday afternoon, and she didn't seem like herself. We both know she wouldn't have done anything to harm Damian, but perhaps someone thinks that she did."

"She was completely infatuated with that man. She never would have hurt him. In her own mind, she believed she loved him."

Connie thought about Maxine's words. If Dottie was that obsessed with Damian, would she have killed him if he rejected her? If Dottie had already been banned from going backstage at Damian's request, perhaps she took that as a rejection and sought revenge on Damian.

But that didn't explain the note. She needed to find out what was in that note and who gave it to Dottie.

After talking with Maxine, Connie glanced at the clock in the lobby and seeing that it was after 6:00, she made a mad dash out of the theatre. Company was due at 6:30 for the tree decorating party. Thank goodness they had already bought the tree and her family was at home preparing the meal. All Connie had to do was show up.

It turned out she didn't need to rush home after all, because everything was under control, so Connie took Ginger for a walk. It was nice having so many enthusiastic hands on deck to help with Ginger, but Connie missed her frequent walks.

By the time she returned home, Greg and Gary had assembled the tree and laid out the garland and ornaments for the festivities, while the scent of manicottis baking in the oven spread through the condo.

Elyse, Josh, Gertrude, Emma, and Victoria arrived first, followed by Grace, Stephanie, and Zach. With her parents, Gianna, Gary, and the twins, it was the most company she had had since she inherited the condo.

Fortunately, the open concept layout left space for an extra folding table, which Connie brought up from her storage bin, to extend her dining room table and accommodate the extra people. Her mother had been right. Everyone fit just fine.

Within no time, dinner was on the table, and everyone was enjoying one another's company.

"We heard that you are the lead investigator on this case," Jo said when there was a lull in the conversation.

"Mom, Zach probably can't talk about the case," Gianna said. "Let him enjoy his manicottis in peace."

"I'm sorry, Zach," Jo said. "I was just making conversation."

Connie looked down to hide a smile. She doubted that was the case.

"That's okay, Mrs. Petretta. Gianna's right. I can't get into the details, but I can tell you we are working hard to follow up on every lead."

"Please, Zach, call me Jo."

He smiled and nodded.

"Do you know if Dottie McKenzie is still missing?" Connie asked. She thought maybe if she kept her questions vague Zach might reveal something.

"Yes. It looks like she doesn't want to be found. Since we have no reason to take her into custody, it's her prerogative to leave town."

Zach and Josh steered the conversation away from the case, so they moved on to other topics.

After clearing the table, at the children's persistent urgings, they gathered in the living room to work on the tree. But not before Greg organized the Christmas grab.

"Since everyone here will also be present for Christmas Day, now is the perfect time to do a grab. I've already written everyone's names down, and they are in this hat," he said, pulling out a baseball cap filled with folded pieces of paper. "Everyone's name is in here, except the children's, since they will get plenty of gifts from everyone, anyway."

Greg passed around the hat, and each person drew a name. Connie picked her brother-in-law, Gary. She'd be sure to elicit some help from Gianna.

A warm feeling spread across Connie's chest as she watched the twins and Victoria playing together, with Emma helping to keep them entertained. While Connie was watching them, Elyse came and stood next to her.

"Emma is great with the little ones," Connie said. "She seems to have gotten over her initial resentment over Victoria joining the family."

"Thankfully, it looks like that is all in the past," Elyse said. "She has grown into a generous and attentive big sister." Emma had been an only child for eleven years before Victoria came to live with the Millers last April. She initially had some trouble adjusting, but Connie was happy to see how well the young family was doing.

"We are expecting the adoption to be final very soon," Elyse said. "Even though she is already our daughter in every other sense of the word."

Connie squeezed Elyse's arm. "It's going to be soon. I can feel it."

With so many helping hands, the tree was decorated in no time. A wave of nostalgia washed over Connie as she thought of her last Christmas tree in her condo in Massachusetts. It may have been a different tree, but the ornaments were the same – a few she had made in elementary school, some to commemorate various vacations she had taken over the years, and two new snowflake ornaments that the twins had made that week. She gave a special spot to a sand dollar ornament with the words "Marco Island" painted on it, which she had bought a couple of years before while on vacation with Concetta, Grace, and her best friend Bethany, who was now living in Colorado with her new husband, Jamie.

After her company left and the cleanup was complete, Connie was still wide awake. She wasn't sure if it was the excitement of having her family and new friends together, especially Zach, or the sugar from too much dessert pumping through her veins, but she didn't want the evening to end.

"I'm too wound up to sleep," Connie said to Gianna and Gary after her parents retired for the night. "I think I'll take Ginger for another walk."

"I'll come with you," Gianna said. "Some fresh air before bed sounds nice."

It was a cool evening, so they each threw on a warm sweatshirt and strolled along the boulevard in the direction of downtown.

Gianna inhaled deeply the crisp, salty air. "I want to take in as much of this as I can. The Farmer's Alamac is predicting a snowy winter."

"You know you're always welcome here."

Gianna smiled and nodded. "I really like Zach. I'm glad you have a second date with him on Sunday night."

"It's been a long time coming. Our first date was so long ago that I was beginning to think it would never happen. In hindsight, we were both at a crossroads, so I guess we needed the time."

"Does it bother him that you are always getting involved in his cases?"

Connie laughed. "I think he's used to that by now. He does worry about me, though, which is nice."

They stopped for a moment to let Ginger sniff some shrubs, then continued down the boulevard.

"Zach didn't seem anxious to locate Dottie," Gianna said. "Do you think that means the police think she's innocent?"

Connie shrugged her shoulders. "She must still be on their list of suspects, but as Zach said, until they have enough evidence to make an arrest, she has every right to leave town."

"I think someone in the cast was on to her, so she ran away to permanently escape justice."

"Or then again," Connie said, "she could have figured out who the killer was and run away for her own safety."

Gianna looked down and smiled as they continued to walk.

"What's so funny?"

"Ever since you moved to Sapphire Beach, I've hated knowing that you were playing amateur sleuth," Gianna said. "But now I understand how you keep getting sucked into these cases. They are hard to let go of, especially when you have a vested interest."

"I know the police are handling things, but Auntie Concetta's connection to the playhouse and our connection to her give us an insider's view. People trust us, because we are her family."

"Besides," Gianna added, "Damian was murdered at the opening of a play dedicated to our aunt's memory. It's hard to sit back and do nothing."

"I'm glad you get it." Connie put an arm around her sister's shoulder. "I'd love to talk to some of our suspects again to see what they think about Dottie's disappearance."

"How are we going to manage that? We're running out of excuses to stop by the playhouse."

"I think I have an idea. Can you and Mom break away about 9:30 tomorrow morning? Grace will be working, and I think I have a good excuse to meet up with some of our suspects before the matinee show."

"Consider it done."

Chapter 13

THE FOLLOWING MORNING, when Connie picked up Gianna in front of the main entrance to Palm Paradise, she was happy to see her mother with her.

"The guys are doing a lot of babysitting this trip," Connie said. "We owe them big."

"Oh, please," Gianna said, waving her hand at Connie. "They're at the beach having a great time. They're happy to be excluded from 'our shenanigans,' as they've dubbed our sleuthing."

"So, what's our plan, Connie?" Jo asked.

"Yeah," Gianna said from the backseat of Connie's Jetta. "What's our excuse for stopping by the playhouse yet again?"

"Take a look on the seat next to you," Connie said as they turned onto Sapphire Beach Boulevard.

"These are Auntie Concetta's scrapbooks," Gianna said, flipping through one of the binders.

"Bingo. I brought most of her scrapbooks home to Mom after I cleaned out the condo in January, but when I realized I was going to relocate, I kept a few here as keepsakes. These two were from the productions they did at the Sapphire Beach Playhouse throughout 2014 and 2015. I had Rick's phone number from the Christmas party when he asked me to call him if I could find the keys, and he said that the cast would love to see them."

"Brilliant," Gianna said. "That's the perfect excuse to assemble most of our suspects together." Gianna flipped through the pages of one of the books. "Actually, *I'm* enjoying seeing them. Here's Sophie and William. It looks like they starred in a show together in 2015. Now that we've had a chance to meet some of the actors, I recognize a lot of people in here." Gianna continued to peruse the scrapbook, giving a narration of each page as she did. Toward the end of the book she stopped on one of the pages. "That's strange."

"What's strange?" Jo asked.

"Here's a picture of Dottie backstage with the cast. It must be just before a performance, because she's wearing her 'Sapphire Beach Playhouse' blazer. She's just hanging out in the background staring at Damian and looking all gaga."

"I guess she's had a crush on him for a long time," Jo said.

They pulled into the theatre parking lot two and a half hours before the play was due to start, so the actors would have time to meet with them before getting into costume and makeup. The trio made their way into the theatre and went backstage, where Connie had arranged to meet Rick.

"Connie, Jo, Gianna – glad you made it," Rick said, waving them over to where he and Sophie were standing together. Rick seemed unusually exuberant.

Sophie embraced all three women. "Rick called to let me know you were coming by with a couple of Concetta's famous scrapbooks, so I just had to come and see them."

"I was hoping you would be here," Jo said. "There are pictures of you and Damian in both albums."

"I also came to personally congratulate Rick," Sophie said. "He has been appointed the interim executive director of the Sapphire Beach Playhouse, with the potential of it becoming a permanent position. The Board of Directors couldn't have made a better choice."

Rick beamed. "Thank you, Sophie. Your support means more than you could know."

So that's why Rick was so happy. Connie couldn't help but wonder how Sophie could share in his joy after he tried to steal her husband's job while he was still alive.

They were joined by Eloise, Stevie, William, and Judith, as well as a handful of other actors whom Connie had seen at the party but hadn't officially met.

Connie discretely observed Sophie and Eloise for any trace of hard feelings between the two women, given Eloise's history with Damian. She remembered the tension between them the night of the Christmas party, but this morning, there was no indication of animosity. Sophie had either moved past her negative feelings toward Eloise or was hiding them well.

From Connie's perspective, that meant one of two things: Either her husband's death had taught her that life is too short for grudges, or the reason that she didn't hold anything over Rick or Eloise was because she was the one who killed Damian.

They walked down the long corridor that led from the theatre into the administrative offices, and everyone gathered in the boardroom – the same boardroom where Connie and her father had hidden from Rick and Priscilla when they broke into the offices last Saturday night. Connie's thoughts must have been written on her face, because her mother and sister were smirking in her direction.

Everyone gathered on one side of the table, so they could look through the pictures together.

As they came to photos that were special to someone, they would stop to reminisce or tell a relevant story. Connie was honored to be brought into their world, even for a few minutes, and relished the opportunity to share this part of her aunt's life. Judging from their expressions, her mother and sister felt the same way.

"Here's a photo of Dottie taken backstage before one of your performances," Connie pointed out. "If this photo is any indication, she's been a fan Damian for a while."

"Oh, yes... Dottie," Sophie said, rolling her eyes. "She was forever finding new ways to 'run into' him before and after performances."

"I still don't understand why she was never barred from the theatre if she was that bad," Jo wondered.

Eloise scoffed. "Good question. I never understood why Damian didn't have her fired. That is, if you can be fired from a volunteer position. She was always poking her nose where it didn't belong."

Rick shifted uncomfortably as Sophie spoke.

Connie, Jo, and Gianna exchanged a curious glance. What was up with Rick?

After they had finished looking through the scrapbooks, Eloise excused herself and Stevie. Connie guessed it was because she didn't want Stevie to hear them discussing the investigation. The boy was such a professional that it was easy to forget he was so young.

"I agree," William said, after Stevie and Eloise left. "I saw Dottie backstage the night of Damian's murder."

"I am confident that the police will uncover the truth," Sophie said. "I know you all mean well, but William, if you told the police that she was backstage, I'm sure they will interview her."

"I did tell the police," William said. "Sophie's right. We should leave the speculation to the police."

Since the actors had a matinee performance to prepare for, they soon left to get ready, and Connie, Jo, and Gianna were alone with Rick.

Now that they had his complete attention, Connie could probe.

"I know from my encounters with Damian that he was a warm and kind person, but that doesn't explain why he would allow Dottie to get away with stalking him backstage," Connie said. "Why didn't he ever put a stop to it? We heard he was planning to talk to you about the situation."

Rick hesitated.

"What aren't you telling us?" Jo asked.

Rick let out a deep sigh. "I never had Dottie barred from the theatre, because Damian asked me not to."

"Why would he do that?" Connie asked. "Did he feel bad for her?"

"I don't think it was that. I saw them talking in the parking lot one night after a show. They appeared to be deep in conversation. I thought it was strange but just shrugged it off. As you said, Damian had a warm personality, and I figured he might have simply been showing her kindness. A couple of days later, Dottie was backstage after the show, and Sophie insisted that she leave. I personally escorted her back to the lobby, and when I came back, Damian pulled me aside and told me to allow her backstage whenever she wanted. He also asked me not to tell the others, which put me in an awkward spot."

"Why on earth would he say that?" Gianna asked.

Rick just shrugged. "I really don't know. But he was the executive director, so he called the shots."

Connie's first thought was that they were having some type of secret affair. Then she shook that idea from her head. Judging from Sophie and Eloise, there was no way that Dottie was Damian's type. Was Dottie blackmailing Damian with something that would cause him to protect her?

"I know a few more people who would love to see these books," Rick said. "Is it okay if we hold onto them for a few more days?"

"Of course," Connie said, handing him the scrapbooks.

"Thank you. I'd better get ready for the show," Rick said and left the room.

The women walked back down the hallway to exit through the theatre and passed by Sophie, who was chatting with someone in the lobby. She finished her conversation as Connie, Jo, and Gianna were leaving, and the four women walked out together.

"Are you staying for the play?" Jo asked.

"I'll be back. I thought I'd run some errands first, since it doesn't start for a couple of hours."

"It seems like everyone is getting along well," Connie said.

"I think it's better that way. While it's true that any one of them could be my husband's killer, as I said inside, I trust that the police will eventually get to the bottom of this. Besides," she added, "I don't want to give the impression that I'm snooping around. I want to stay safe."

Given all she had been through, Sophie's plan was probably a prudent one. But still, Connie didn't understand how she could be so diplomatic when she might have been in the presence of her husband's murderer.

"What did you think of all that?" Jo asked her daughters as they drove home.

"It doesn't make sense that Damian would protect Dottie and allow her backstage when she was clearly a nuisance," Gianna said.

"What could have happened that would cause Damian to change his behavior toward her?" Gianna asked.

"Whatever it was, it could be connected to why he was killed," Jo said.

"And it also might be connected to the reason she ran away," Connie said. "Only Dottie knows, and she's nowhere to be found."

Chapter 14

BY THE TIME CONNIE made it back to *Just Jewelry* with Ginger in tow, it was late Saturday morning. Her first order of business was to check on the progress of Operation Chicken Coop. With only three shopping days left until Christmas Eve, if they didn't sell out soon, they wouldn't make their goal. She took inventory and determined that there were just over fifty pairs of earrings left to sell. It was doable, but there was no guarantee they would pull it off.

Since Grace had everything under control in the shop, Connie decided to take Ginger for a walk around town before what she anticipated would be a busy afternoon. Connie and Ginger wandered in the direction of the pier and came across Gallagher

McKeon, who was nursing a cup of coffee on his favorite bench facing the beach. Gallagher was her friend and the owner of *Gallagher's Tropical Shack*, a restaurant across the street from *Just Jewelry,* whose thatched roof and beachy motif added a tropical ambiance to Connie's view.

Connie joined Gallagher on the bench.

"I met your family the other day when they came into the restaurant for dinner," Gallagher said. "I heard two little ones talking about their 'Auntie Connie', so I guessed they were referring to you and introduced myself. They are absolutely adorable."

A smile spread across Connie's face at the thought of her niece and nephew. "My parents told me that you sat with them for a while. I'm so happy that you were able to meet them. I told them that you are a friend and made them promise to stop in and introduce themselves. You must have beat them to it."

"Your mother is so kind. She invited me to Christmas dinner, but the restaurant will be open, so I had to decline. But I did promise to try to stop by for dessert later in the day."

"That would be wonderful. If Penelope is free, tell her to come, as well."

Just after Connie finished speaking, out of the corner of her eye she noticed a sudden movement in the direction of the pier. The short, dark hair and energetic stride looked familiar. Was that Dottie? She had to find out. Now might be her only chance to find out why she disappeared.

"I'll be right back," Connie said as she handed off Ginger's leash to a confused Gallagher and followed the woman, who was now heading away from the pier and down the beach at a brisk pace. Connie stayed close behind her as she navigated the beach blankets and sidestepped the stream of beachgoers playing and walking on the beach. The woman scanned her options, then made a sharp turn up the wooden stairs and onto the deck of *Surfside Restaurant*.

Connie did her best to shorten the gap between them, but with so many people out and about, it was hard to make much progress. Connie followed her onto the *Surfside* deck and into the indoor dining area, attempting to avoid the dark green plastic tables and chairs in her way. When the woman reached the

167

dining room, she stopped to glance behind her and looked right at Connie.

It was definitely Dottie.

Her eyes seemed to contain more fear than guilt. Dottie turned and bolted out of the restaurant. Connie arrived at the front entrance about ten seconds after Dottie. She scanned the shop-lined pedestrian street in every direction, but Dottie had too much of a head start. She was nowhere to be found. Connie entered a few of the nearby shops, thinking she might have ducked into one of them, but no luck. She was gone.

Connie clenched her fists in frustration and went back to get Ginger.

"What was that all about?" Gallagher asked.

"I thought I saw someone I knew, but I wasn't able to catch up with her," Connie said. It was at least partly true. She just didn't mention that Dottie clearly didn't want to be caught up with.

Gallagher smiled playfully at Connie. "Let me get this straight. I happen to know you attended the opening performance of 'A Christmas Carol,' where a murder took place, and now you take off chasing someone across the beach. There's no way you'll convince me and Ginger here that there's no connection," he said, handing Connie back the leash. "We know better."

"Okay, I won't try to convince either of you." There was no point in trying to fool Gallagher. He had her number.

"Just be careful, my friend. As you know from experience, killers are dangerous."

"I know. I promise."

Connie thanked Gallagher for watching Ginger, then headed back to *Just Jewelry* to get ready for the afternoon rush.

On her way back, Connie stopped at Ruby's souvenir shop, located next door to *Just Jewelry*. Ruby carried a few Fair Trade products made by Connie's artisans. The items, which included purses, wallets, beach bags, and handbags were selling well, and Connie had been meaning to check and see if she needed more inventory.

It turned out Ruby's inventory was indeed running low, especially her supply of beach bags from Kenya, so Ruby placed an order to replenish her stock. Dura would be pleased. The more items Connie ordered, the busier Dura was able to keep her artisans, and additional orders even allowed her to hire and train new ones, providing much-needed income to an area desperately in need of employment opportunities. Since Ruby's shop sold mainly t-shirts, sweatshirts, and other Sapphire Beach memorabilia, Dura had created a special line of beach bags with the words "Sapphire Beach" embroidered on them, as well as other tropical designs, which were doing well with Ruby's clientele.

"How is your fundraiser going?" Ruby asked.

"We've sold a lot of earrings in the past couple of weeks, but I wish we had started earlier. We still have about fifty more to go to make our goal."

"Say no more," Ruby said. "I probably can't sell as many as you, since we have a different clientele, but with some gentle prodding, I think I could sell some. They make wonderful Christmas gifts, and they are for a great cause. I'd be happy to keep some next to the cash register and talk them up while people are checking out."

Connie was so excited that she hugged Ruby. "You're the best neighbor, Ruby. That is so kind of you."

"God has been good to me. It's the least I can do to give back."

Connie returned to *Just Jewelry*, arranged some earrings in a small basket, and printed and framed a sign detailing the project for Ruby to display. Since Grace and Ruby had become good friends, Grace happily volunteered to bring everything over to Ruby's shop before leaving for the day.

Being the Saturday before Christmas, the shop was bustling with activity all day. The energy on the downtown streets was palpable, and Connie enjoyed gazing out the front window, observing shoppers in action. More than a few men of various ages came into the shop, looking for gifts for their significant other. Connie enjoyed asking questions about the recipient's taste and helping them choose the perfect gift. The Fair Trade jewelry was selling well, too. People were eager to buy gifts that would help to employ those in need. Soon, Connie would have to send another jewelry order to Dura and her other artisans.

There was a brief lull in the middle of the afternoon. Judging from the line at *Gallagher's*, Connie guessed shoppers were taking a late lunch or an early dinner. She sat down on the sofa in the seating area to rest her feet and was pleasantly surprised to see Elyse walk in.

Connie jumped up to greet her friend. "What a wonderful surprise."

"Josh is watching the girls while I sneak out to do some last-minute Christmas shopping," Elyse said, examining one of the jewelry displays. "Actually, my mother is the last person on my list, and I think these would be perfect for her." She held up a teal necklace and bracelet made in Ecuador. "She will really appreciate that they are Fair Trade."

After Connie rang up Elyse's purchase, she caught her up to speed on her latest investigative activities.

"You've been keeping busy," Elyse said. "I can't believe your mother and sister are helping you. They have always been so against your getting involved in these things."

"I know, right? But since Damian was a friend of my aunt's, it's hard not to get involved."

"You might not have to wait much longer for justice. Josh said that they are getting close to making an arrest."

"Are you serious?" Connie asked. "Do you know who?"

"He didn't say, and I don't usually ask."

"I guess we'll know soon enough. Thanks for letting me know."

Elyse held up the box with the jewelry she just purchased and smiled. "And thanks for helping me finish my Christmas shopping."

"Anytime," Connie said. "I'll see you on Christmas Day, if not before."

When Abby arrived for her Saturday evening shift, she practically pushed Connie out of the shop. "Go," she said. "I'm flying home to Indiana on Monday for Christmas break, so this weekend is your last chance to take evenings off until I return in January."

"Are you sure, Abby? I'm taking tomorrow evening off for my date with Zach."

"Positive. Go enjoy your family while you can."

When Connie got home, there was nobody there; however, it didn't take long to locate them. She stepped onto the balcony, and as she scanned the beach below, just beyond the pool area, she discovered her mom and Gary playing with the twins, while Gianna and her dad tossed a frisbee. Connie smiled at the sight.

She grabbed a light sweatshirt, since it was cooling off, and walked around the building onto the silky white sand.

The twins were the first to spot her and ran in her direction. She wrestled them onto the sand, then carried them toward the blanket, holding one in each arm.

"You two are getting so big," she said, collapsing onto the blanket. "I'm not going to be able to do that for much longer."

The others came over to join Connie and the twins.

"Honey, what a pleasant surprise," Jo said, giving her a hug. "We thought you were working."

"I decided to play hooky tonight while I can, before Abby goes home for Christmas."

Once the sun began to set, they went upstairs to share a dinner of baked chicken, broccoli, and ziti alfredo, which Gianna had prepared, and spent the evening further catching up on one another's lives. Connie heard all about the twins' adventures in preschool, Jo's and Gianna's booming home staging

174

business, Greg's accounting business, and Gary's physical therapy practice.

It wasn't until the twins were finally in bed that Connie filled the others in on her near run-in with Dottie and on Elyse's news that the police were close to making an arrest.

"Are you sure it was Dottie?" Gianna asked. "Why would she run away from you of all people?"

"I don't know," Connie said, "but for a moment I looked right into her eyes. I'm telling you, she looked more scared than guilty."

"I guess we'll know soon enough, if the police make an arrest," Greg said. "I, for one, will be happy to see this case resolved so I no longer have to worry about the three of you getting into trouble."

Chapter 15

ON SUNDAY MORNING, the whole family woke up early to attend the 7:00 Mass at Our Lady, Star of the Sea with Connie. She had told Fr. Paul Fulton about the chicken coop project in passing a couple of weeks ago, and, to Connie's delight, he had placed a notice in the bulletin informing people of the fundraising project taking place at *Just Jewelry*. She could have hugged him when her father pointed out the announcement, which encouraged parishioners to support the worthy cause.

With only a couple of days left until Christmas, the publicity came just in time.

After Mass, Connie and her family went out to breakfast, then Connie headed to the shop.

The first two customers of the day were women that Connie recognized from Mass.

"Hi ladies," Connie said. "Didn't I see you at church this morning?"

"We heard Fr. Paul's announcement about your fundraiser," one of the women said. She held up a pair of candy cane earrings she had taken from one of the displays. "Are these the earrings he was talking about? They are just beautiful."

"Thank you," Connie said. "Yes. And they are all handmade."

Each woman purchased five pairs. "I'm going to give one to each of my daughters and my sister and keep one for myself," the first woman said.

"I'm going to give them to some friends. I'm always looking for meaningful gifts that don't cost an arm and a leg, and these are just perfect," the other said.

After ringing up their purchases, Connie gave them each a flyer with information on the nutrition center project and took their email addresses. She had been collecting the names and email addresses of those who purchased a pair of candy cane earrings, if they wished to leave it, so that she could send pictures of the project when it was complete and inform them of future projects.

All morning, people popped in, occasionally from the parish, to purchase earrings. For the first time all weekend, Connie was confident that they would reach their goal by Christmas Eve. When Grace arrived, she went over to Ruby's to check on her progress. Ruby had sold twelve pairs, and Grace picked up the extras. There were only sixteen pairs left to sell.

Abby arrived early for her shift so that Connie could get ready for her date with Zach that evening. As Connie was getting into her car to head home, her phone pinged with a text from Gianna. *Can you come home? It's Mom.*

Connie's heart raced as she shot off a quick reply. *I'm on my way.*

The one-mile drive home seemed like ten as Connie's thoughts leapt to every negative conclusion. Her mother had just barely turned sixty, and she was in good health. Maybe the stress of running the business with Gianna was beginning to take its toll. If both Connie and Gianna had a heart-to-heart

179

conversation with their mother, maybe she would consider cutting back on hours.

Connie punched in the access code to the underground garage and pulled into her designated spot. It felt like the elevator took an eternity to arrive and take her to the seventh floor. When the door finally opened, she practically ran down the hallway and burst through the door that led into her unit. She was surprised to see Zach sitting in the living room with her family. It didn't appear to be a social call.

Her father had his arm around her mother's shoulders, with Gianna and Gary sitting on the other side of Jo. Gianna was holding her mother's hand and comforting her.

"What's going on?" Connie asked.

Gary stood up and handed Connie his phone.

"Your mom was at the flea market doing a little shopping, and when she returned to her car, this note was on the windshield."

Gary's phone displayed a picture of a note that read, *If you know what's best for you and your daughters, you will mind your own business or you will end up like Damian.*

It wasn't the first time Connie was threatened as a result of her sleuthing, but this one involved her mother and her sister. This one crossed a line.

"Mom, did you see anyone you knew at the flea market? Somebody from the playhouse maybe?"

Jo shook her head. "No. I wasn't there for that long. I just popped in to pick up a pair of sunglasses and a battery for my watch. After that, I got an ice cream cone and headed back to my car."

"The person was likely following you," Zach said, "since they knew which car was yours."

"You ladies need to take heed of that note," Greg said.

"I agree," Gary added. "You've clearly done something to hit a nerve. This person has already killed once. You need to leave the investigating to the police."

"I doubt whoever left the note would be dumb enough to leave fingerprints on it, but I'll have the letter checked for prints, anyway," Zach said. "Connie, are you still up for going out tonight?"

Connie hesitated. The last thing she wanted to do was cancel her date with Zach. After all, it took them nearly eight months after their first date to finally schedule a second one. She was afraid if it didn't happen tonight, it would never happen. But she also hated the thought of leaving her mother's side at a time like this.

"Of course she is," Jo said. "We'll be fine here."

"And if Connie is going to be out tonight, I feel better knowing she will be with a police officer," her father said.

Zach looked at Connie for confirmation.

She reluctantly nodded in agreement.

"It's settled then," Zach said. "I have to drop the letter off at the station, then go home to change. How about if I pick you up in an hour and a half?"

"Perfect," Connie said. "I'll meet you in the lobby at 4:00."

Greg insisted on accompanying Connie while she walked Ginger, so Connie humored him. She doubted the killer would make two dramatic moves in one day. He or she was trying to scare the women away from the case and would likely wait to see what affect the first threat had before trying something else.

When they returned upstairs, Connie took a shower and got ready for her date with Zach. She chose a casual hunter green dress with a light cream-colored sweater, since evenings could be cool this time of year. It might have been her imagination, but Connie could have sworn her blood was thinning out already from the warm Florida weather. She found herself wearing a light sweater in the evenings, even when her family didn't seem to require one. She also chose a lightweight necklace made with genuine seashells and a matching bracelet.

Gianna went downstairs to keep Connie company while she waited for Zach in the lobby. They sat in two oversized chairs by the Christmas tree, which had red Christmas berry branches scattered throughout for decoration.

"Judging from how you've operated in the past, I know the note Mom got isn't going to deter you," Gianna said.

Gianna was right. The note had the opposite effect on Connie. Now that the killer involved her mother and her sister, she was more determined than ever to see to it that he or she was behind bars. "There's nothing I hate more than a bully. We must have the killer scared if he or she is resorting to threats."

"You had a run-in with Dottie shortly before Mom received the note. If she's the killer, you might have scared her."

"I was thinking that, too," Connie said. "But we were also at the playhouse recently with the scrapbooks asking questions."

"I won't try to convince you to stay out of it, because I know that when you make up your mind to do something, there is no stopping you. Just promise that if you sense that you're in any danger, you will let someone know."

Connie crossed her heart with her index finger. "I promise."

"The berry branches in this Christmas tree made me think of something I've been meaning to tell you," Gianna said. "I was doing some research and, did you know that Christmas berries contain cyanide?"

"I didn't," Connie said. "But what does that have to do with anything?"

"The tree in the lobby of the theatre is decorated with Christmas berries, just like this one," Gianna said. "Maybe the killer used the berries to poison Damian."

Connie had to laugh. "I think Damian would have noticed if his antacid was red. And besides, we saw the bottle in his dressing room the night of his murder, and some of its contents had dripped down the side. It was definitely white, remember?"

Gianna leaned back in her chair, looking disappointed. "I suppose you're right. I thought maybe I was on to something."

Zach drove into the parking lot in his gray Jeep, and Connie waved to Gianna on her way out.

"Have fun," Gianna said. "I want details tonight."

As they merged onto Route 75 South towards Naples, Connie realized how much she was looking forward to leaving behind her stress and enjoying some Christmas festivities with Zach. They cruised down the highway, leaving Sapphire Beach behind, and all the tension melted from Connie's shoulders. The timing of their date turned out to be perfect.

The plan was to explore the neighborhood, find a restaurant for dinner, and check out the infamous artificial snow, which fell nightly at 7:00 on Third Street South. They had also planned a bit of last-minute Christmas shopping for the grab. It turned out

Zach drew Gianna's name, and since Connie had Gary, they agreed to help one another choose gifts.

Zach parked in a garage near Third Street South, then they headed off to explore a little corner of Naples. Palm trees tightly wrapped in white lights greeted them as they emerged from the parking garage. As they strolled toward a more populated area, they passed a majestic ivory staircase decorated in garland and giant wreaths. They stopped to take a selfie at a massive Christmas tree with lights bouncing off gigantic red and gold bulbs.

"Let's find a restaurant," Connie suggested. "It's early, but I have a feeling there will be a long wait. We should get our name in somewhere."

As they perused several menus posted in front of outdoor patios, Christmas carols streamed through the sound systems of the restaurants where they stopped. Many people were eating outside, and there was a palpable festive energy. It was different from what Connie was accustomed to back in New England, but charming in its own unique fashion. It was like being in the north pole, but with palm trees and warm weather. A few minutes into their explorations, Connie became aware of how natural it felt sharing the moment with Zach.

After some deliberation, they settled on a bistro with plenty of outdoor seating and several dishes they both liked. Zach put his name in for a reservation and was given a beeper. They were promised a table in about a forty-five minutes, so they sat on a nearby bench to wait.

Chapter 16

AS CONNIE AND ZACH waited for their table, she caught him up on her family's stay in Sapphire Beach. "It will be hard to see them leave on Friday."

"Does it give you any regrets about moving so far away?"

Connie sighed. It had been hard to make the decision to leave Massachusetts and relocate nearly a year ago, but once she finally did there were no regrets. "I'm not going to say it's easy, but I feel like Sapphire Beach is where I'm supposed to be."

Zach looked at her thoughtfully. "I don't think there is any time or place in life that is perfect. I've actually been thinking a lot about that lately – how happiness doesn't come all at once. You have a piece here and a piece there, but no place or time in our life ever contains everything."

Connie reflected for a moment. "You know, I think you're right. When I lived in Africa, my life was full of exciting adventures and new friends, but I missed everyone back home. When I returned home, I loved my job and being near family, but after a while, I needed a new challenge. Here in Sapphire Beach I have a beautiful home, my Fair Trade work and a creative outlet in my jewelry making, but my family is far, and my aunt Concetta and others I've loved are no longer with us."

"That's exactly what I mean. I guess we need to focus on today's blessings instead of what we're missing. Perfect joy is for heaven, not earth."

"I like that," Connie said. She had almost forgotten how much she loved this contemplative side of Zach, which he revealed more when they were alone. "How about you? Any regrets since you made the decision to stay?" Connie was referring to last July when Zach received a job offer in his hometown but ultimately decided not to take it.

He smiled. "No regrets. I just had to go through the process of deciding once and for all that Sapphire

Beach was home. Besides, if I hadn't stayed, I'd be missing out on tonight," he said, taking Connie's hand. Just as he folded his hand around hers, the beeper went off, startling them both.

"It looks like our table is ready," Connie said, laughing.

The hostess led them to a wonderful, out-of-the-way table overlooking Third Avenue South. Connie ordered chicken cordon bleu, and Zach ordered a New York sirloin.

"How is your house hunting going?" Connie asked, after they placed their order.

Zach's blue eyes grew bright with excitement. "Elyse has been showing me a lot of properties, and I think I've narrowed down where I'd like to be. I'm drawn to the bungalows in the streets that run perpendicular to the boulevard. I love those quiet little neighborhoods off the beaten path. My dream is to be on a canal, but even though I've been saving for a long time, I don't know if I'll be able to afford one of those."

"Maybe you could get a fixer upper at a good price," Connie suggested.

"You never know. I'll see what comes on the market in the next couple of months."

"Stephanie bought one of those bungalows a few years ago. Elyse and I spend a lot of time hanging out there. Stephanie's bungalow isn't on a canal, but it has a fantastic lanai."

"I'd be happy with something like that, too. Now that I know what I want, Elyse has some showings lined up, so I'm optimistic that it's only a matter of time until I find the right place."

Although there had been a lot of obstacles to overcome before Connie and Zach's second date, the wait had brought with it certain advantages, among them the opportunity for their friendship to develop. Their conversation flowed, and dinner flew by. By the time Zach paid the check, it was nearly time for the snow.

Connie and Zach gathered with families and people of all ages, anxiously awaiting the snow. Cheers erupted from the small crowed as a grinding sound from the pumps above gradually grew louder until thick white, foam fell on the people.

Children ran towards the faux snow, now gathering on the street. When the coast was clear of running children, Connie and Zach went closer to touch the white substance. It reminded Connie of a very light shaving cream. She couldn't resist grabbing a handful and throwing it into Zach's clean-cut blond hair.

"Now you asked for it," he said, filling his hands with snow and dropping it on her head.

Connie flinched, half expecting the foamy substance to be cold as it dripped from her dark hair and landed on her dress.

Zach laughed as he pushed a strand of hair out of her eyes and tucked it behind her ear. She slipped her arms around his waist as he kissed her. She could get used to that.

When they stepped apart, Connie wiped off the snow that had gathered on her head, since unlike real snow, it didn't melt.

"Why don't we get our shopping done before the stores close?" Connie suggested. "I noticed some shops that looked promising on our way from the garage to the restaurant."

They retraced their earlier steps, and as they passed the bench they had been sitting on earlier,

Connie stopped short. She couldn't believe her eyes. Sitting on the same bench was Dottie McKenzie.

For a moment, Dottie was speechless as she noticed Connie and Zach standing in front of her. She couldn't run away this time.

"Shoot," Dottie said. "I was hoping I wouldn't see anyone I know out here tonight."

Connie and Zach sat on either side of Dottie.

"Everyone is worried about you, Dottie. Why did you run away without telling anyone where you were?" Zach asked.

"Oh, I didn't mean to cause any trouble," Dottie said, waving her hand at Zach. "I figured you would catch the killer sooner or later, and I just felt more comfortable laying low until you made an arrest."

Connie remembered what Maxine had told her, about Dottie receiving a note just before she disappeared. Connie placed her hand on Dottie's arm. "Dottie, why did you feel unsafe? Did someone threaten you?"

She looked at the ground, then back up at Connie. She slowly opened her purse, pulled a note, and with a shaky voice, read it aloud. "I know what you heard on Friday night. You'd better keep quiet or else…"

Zach examined the note. "Do you have any idea who sent it?"

"No. And I have no idea who the killer is."

Connie could hear the anxiety in Dottie's voice, so she tried another approach. "Dottie, why did Damian tell Rick to allow you backstage before the performances?"

Dottie fidgeted with the strap on her purse. "Damian believed that someone wanted to hurt him. He didn't say who, but he knew I liked to come backstage before the performances." Her eyes brightened. "I just love the energy in the air. Going back there and wishing the performers luck, well... it made me feel like I was part of the group. Damian promised he would work it out with Rick so that I wouldn't get into trouble if I would keep an ear out for anything suspicious. Damian said I would be safe, because the other actors would never suspect that I was eavesdropping." Tears filled Dottie's eyes. "Maybe if I had been more successful, Damian wouldn't be dead. I can't help but think that I could have saved him."

Connie fished a tissue from her purse and handed it to Dottie. Then she put an arm around Dottie's shoulders. "It's not your fault, Dottie. Whoever killed Damian was a sick person, and there was nothing you could have done."

"She's right," Zach said. "He should have come to the police, not to you."

"You said that you don't know who killed Damian," Zach said, "but is there anything you did overhear?"

"Just that..." She looked around as if to make sure nobody could overhear them. "I heard Damian fighting with Eloise Lambert. Apparently, Damian was Stevie's biological father, and Damian wanted Eloise to tell Stevie. He said he couldn't keep the secret anymore." Dottie shook her head. "I can't believe I was so infatuated with that man. He is a jerk – first having an affair with Eloise, then wanting to uproot that little boy's life. I hate to speak ill of the dead, but that was a selfish idea." Tears spilled from her eyes. "And now my association with him has gotten me into hot water."

Poor Dottie didn't seem to know how to feel about Damian. She had admired him for so long and now, she was so disappointed in him. "I'm sorry you had to hear that," Connie said.

Dottie's information explained a lot. She had considered Damian a friend, not because she was delusional, but because, in some small way, they *had* become friends. And she didn't think Damian wanted to leave Sophie for her, but for Eloise.

Since Dottie was convinced that the killer thought she knew his or her identity, she insisted on laying low until the police arrested the killer.

Zach took her contact information and assured her that he would let her know if there were any breaks in the case. "Hopefully it won't be long," he said.

Connie and Zach left Dottie so they could do their shopping. Connie helped Zach choose a hand painted serving dish that was just Gianna's taste, and Zach suggested a digital picture frame for Gary. Zach was concerned that his gift would be too cumbersome for Gianna to carry on the airplane, so Connie promised she would ship the dish home for Gianna after she opened it on Christmas day.

"That was a lot easier than I thought it would be," Zach said as they made their way back to the parking garage.

"It's funny how easy it is to spend money," Connie said.

As Connie and Zach drove back to Sapphire Beach, they were both lost in thought. After a few minutes, Connie broke the silence. "It's so strange how Dottie was so wrapped up in Damian Pritchard for so long, even though she barely knew him. She was upset over his indiscretions, as if he were a close friend. It's kind of sad in a way that she would be so concerned about someone she barely knew."

"I guess we all want to feel like we belong somewhere."

All night Connie had been thinking about what Elyse had told her – that the police were getting ready to make an arrest – but since she knew Zach wouldn't be able to talk about it anyway, she didn't bring it up directly.

"Does that mean Dottie is no longer on your list of suspects?" Connie asked instead.

"I think her tears and fear were genuine."

About the only thing that Connie learned for sure that night was that Dottie wasn't the suspect that the police planned to arrest. And based on their conversation, Dottie was off Connie's list, as well.

Zach parked in a visitor parking space at Palm Paradise and walked Connie to the lobby.

"I had a great time," Connie said. "I enjoyed the snow and the company."

"I did too," he said, giving her a gentle kiss.

They lingered in the lobby until the elevator arrived. Then Connie went upstairs.

Chapter 17

CONNIE KNEW HER SISTER and mother would be anxiously awaiting the details of her date, and truth be told, she was eager to talk about it.

Sure enough, they were watching TV with Ginger napping comfortably between them when Connie arrived home. She had to laugh when they both leapt up to greet her. Ginger seemed confused at the excitement but greeted Connie with a wagging tail, anyway.

"Where's Dad and Gary?"

"We gave the guys the night off, since they have been so good about watching the twins. They went down to a sports bar to catch the football game and haven't come home yet."

Jo and Gianna dragged Connie over to the sofa, and Ginger hopped onto her lap. She stroked the dog's silky fur while her mother and sister grilled her on the date.

"Your smile says it all," Jo said.

Connie hadn't realized she was smiling. "Zach's a special guy," Connie said. "I really like him."

After patiently answering all their questions, Connie told her mother and sister about their encounter with Dottie.

"Wow, that's crazy. Did she try to run away this time?" Gianna asked.

"I think she would have, but we didn't give her the chance. Once we finally got her talking, she appeared relieved to get everything off her chest. It turns out that the night Damian was murdered, she overheard a fight between him and Eloise about Stevie. Damian wanted Stevie to know he was his biological father, and Eloise was against telling him for obvious reasons. Dottie insists she doesn't know who the killer is; however, she is convinced that the killer thinks she does."

"Poor Dottie," Jo said. "It's never easy to see an idol fall from grace."

"She was pretty disappointed in him," Connie said. "I felt bad."

"Damian was always kind to my sister, and that's what I choose to focus on," Jo said.

"I agree," Connie said. "And after talking with Dottie tonight, her behavior over the past week and a half makes a lot more sense. I don't think she's the killer."

Gianna was quiet while Connie and Jo discussed the situation. Then she leaned back on the couch and said, "I think Eloise is the killer, and since Dottie overheard her fighting with Damian, she thinks Dottie is onto her."

"You could be right," Connie said.

***

Early Monday afternoon, after a customer left with the last two pairs of candy cane earrings, Connie held two fists high above her head. "I can't believe we sold the last two pairs the day before Christmas Eve. I can't wait to tell Dura the good news."

"Congratulations, honey. I'm so proud of you," Grace said. "I can wait a little while longer for my lunch break if you want to run to the bank. I know you're anxious to get the ball rolling on this project."

"Thanks," Connie said, grabbing her purse and sprinting to the door. "I'll be back in a few."

Connie wasted no time wiring the four thousand dollars to Dura's bank account so they could begin work on the chicken coop as soon as the money cleared. When she returned to the shop, Connie immediately emailed Dura to tell her the good news and alert her that the money was on its way. Then Connie and Grace sat on the couch and enjoyed a glass of lemonade with some celebratory cupcakes that Connie had picked up on her way back.

While they were celebrating, Zach came to the shop and joined their celebration.

Connie handed Zach a plate with a cupcake while Grace poured him a glass of lemonade.

"Thank you," Zach said. "Congratulations on meeting your fundraising goal. I can't wait to see pictures of the project. But I actually stopped by for another reason. I wanted to let you know that we arrested Rick Bennett this morning for Damian Pritchard's murder."

Connie nearly dropped her plate. "Wow, that's huge."

"I wanted to tell you in person, since Damian was a friend of your aunt," Zach said. "It turned out that Rick bought the bottle of antacid that killed Damian and left it in Damian's dressing room. Rick swore the bottle was sealed when he left it there, but we found cyanide in his personal possessions, and only Rick and Damian's fingerprints were on the bottle."

"So, Rick killed Damian to save his job?"

"Damian planned to cut back on the number of performances, and consequently on paid staff, as a last-ditch effort to save the playhouse. He knew it wouldn't be a popular plan, but apparently it was unpopular enough to cost him his life."

Connie put her empty plate on the coffee table. The cupcake now felt like lead in her stomach. "I suppose I should be happy the killer is behind bars, but I still have an uneasy feeling."

"It's probably the shock of learning who the killer is," Zach said. "At least now you can focus on enjoying the rest of your family's visit."

That was true. Connie was relieved to know her family was safe now, especially after the note her mother had received.

Even a couple of minutes after Zach broke the news, Grace sat there with her mouth agape. "It's just so hard to believe Rick is a killer. I've known him for years."

"I'm sorry, Grace," Zach said.

Grace shook her head. "Never mind about that. I'm going to look on the bright side. Today has been a good day. Not only did we meet our fundraising goal, but Damian's killer is behind bars. I'm just so surprised that it turned out to be Rick."

"And Christmas is only two days away," Connie added.

"That's right," Grace said. "Speaking of Christmas, I have a last-minute gift that I need to pick up on my lunch break. I'll be back in an hour."

Since Abby had flown out that morning and the store would be closed on Christmas Day, Grace agreed to work a few extra hours to keep Connie company.

"Does Rick's arrest mean that Dottie is coming out of hiding?" Connie asked after Grace left.

Zach nodded. "Not only that, I called a few hours ago to give her the news, and she said she was excited to return to the playhouse for the Christmas Eve performance."

"That's good news," Connie said.

Zach smiled at Connie.

"Was there something else?" she asked, returning his smile.

"Well... maybe. I didn't *just* come by to update you on the case. I wanted you to know how much I enjoyed our date last night."

Connie felt her smile becoming broader. "I did, too."

"Perhaps we can go out again after the holidays."

Her heartbeat felt like it doubled in speed. "I'd like that."

Zach returned to work, and for the rest of the day Connie tried to remain focused, but an image of Rick Bennett in prison kept pushing its way into her thoughts. Both Sophie and Grace's friend, Peter Holloway, said that Rick had been vying for Damian's job. Now that Damian was gone, Rick had been named interim executive director with the possibility of it becoming a permanent position. The promotion probably came with a nice pay raise, as well. If Rick's motive was to save his job, his plan had worked perfectly... until he got caught.

It *had* to be Rick. He had been on Connie's list of suspects all along. So, why was doubt gnawing at the back of her mind? Maybe it was because it didn't seem likely that a director would kill his lead actor on the opening night of a performance. Or because both Eloise and Sophie seemed to have stronger motives. Or perhaps it was the expression of pure shock on Grace's face when she learned the news. Grace was usually a good judge of character.

Whatever the reason, there was nothing Connie could do about it now. Tomorrow was Christmas Eve, one of her favorite nights of the year, and she was determined not to let anything distract her. She couldn't wait to close the shop early tomorrow, have dinner with her family, and go to midnight Mass. Then the following morning, Santa would bring Hannah and Noah all the presents that Gianna and Gary had hidden in their parents' room at Grace's apartment. And the icing on the cake would be when her family and friends gathered in her home for Christmas. She had too much to look forward to. So, what was this uneasy feeling that kept rising inside her like driftwood on a wave?

If Rick didn't do it, who did? The only two suspects that remained on Connie's list were Sophie and Eloise.

"It's quiet out there," Grace said, returning with a shopping bag in hand. "A lot of people must have gone north for the holidays."

Connie had been so lost in her thoughts that she didn't even realize that no customers had come through the door since Grace left an hour before.

Still unable to push the case out of her mind, Connie found herself grabbing her purse and telling Grace she would return in a few minutes.

Chapter 18

AS CONNIE DROVE down Sapphire Beach Boulevard past Palm Paradise and toward Sophie's house, she racked her brain for a believable excuse to pop in. She could invite Sophie over for Christmas Day, but what if it turned out she was a killer?

Bad idea.

The only legitimate reason she could think of was to make sure that Sophie knew Rick had been arrested. It was a weak excuse, but unless she could come up with a better one in the next few minutes, it would have to do.

As Connie's Jetta continued to hug the coastline dotted with mansions, she thought about how she would handle herself. She wouldn't go inside, just in case Sophie was dangerous, but she would try to engage her in a conversation. She doubted Sophie would invite her in the house, anyway, since Sophie always seemed to think her home was a mess.

Lost in thought, Connie refocused her attention on her driving and suddenly realized that the street no longer looked familiar. She must have overshot the house. After making a U-turn and backtracking a short distance, Connie realized why she hadn't seen the Pritchard house. There was a large moving van parked in front, blocking the view from the street. It was Big and Burley movers, the same company that Connie had used to move her furniture from her storage unit to *Just Jewelry* nine months before. Several workers swiftly moved from the mansion into the truck, with boxes and small pieces of furniture in hand, while Sophie sat on a lawn chair staring blankly at all the activity. She looked more like a small child than a criminal.

Connie parked her car a safe distance from the truck and approached Sophie. She seemed oblivious to the fact that Connie was even there.

"Hi, Sophie," Connie said.

She looked up suddenly, then averted her eyes from Connie's questioning gaze.

"Hi, Connie. I guess my secret's out."

Sophie's strange behavior over the past couple of weeks was beginning to make sense – her reaction the night of the Christmas party when Connie almost went into the guest bedroom, thinking it was the bathroom, and Sophie insisting that Connie and her mother and sister visit with her on the lanai. The Pritchards must have been packing and planning to move even before Damian's death.

"Why didn't you tell anyone you were moving? I'm sure your friends at the playhouse would have helped you pack."

Sophie let out a sarcastic chuckle. "I love them, but they are a bunch of busybodies. They would have been more interested in gossiping than helping."

"Maybe not everyone," Connie said. But even as she spoke the words, she wasn't sure if she believed them herself.

"Too many of them. Once the rumor mill gets started, it's hard to shut it down. After I get through this move, I'll make the announcement. At this point, people will probably think I sold because of losing Damian."

"Let them think what they want. Your personal decisions aren't anyone's business, anyway."

"I'm glad you're here, Connie. I wanted to let you know that your aunt's scrapbooks are in the boardroom. Everyone who wants to see them has, so feel free to pick them up at any time."

"Thank you," Connie said. For the second time in two days, Connie discovered that appearances and truth could be two very different things. First Dottie, and now Sophie. Rumors had been circulating that Damian was going to move out and leave Sophie, but that was only half true. Apparently, Damian *was* planning to move out, but they both were. Damian wasn't leaving his wife. He and his wife were simply moving.

"I assume you heard that Rick was arrested," Connie said.

Sophie nodded and gazed off into the distance. "It's ironic that Rick would have killed Damian to save the playhouse. Damian stopped taking a paycheck last year, which is why we couldn't afford to stay on top of our mortgage payment. Damian wanted nothing more than to see that theatre thrive. He did everything he could to avoid layoffs. First, he took a pay cut, then he stopped drawing a salary altogether. We knew that would mean giving up the house eventually, but that's how much we loved that theatre."

"That was very generous of both of you," Connie said.

"We never should have bought this house to begin with. The mortgage and upkeep were a stretch for our budget, even when we bought it ten years ago, and Damian was still getting the occasional acting job. But we got caught up in living the high life. When money got tight, we decided to sell it. It was Damian who insisted on keeping it through the holidays and having one last Christmas party."

"It was a spectacular party," Connie said. "I will always be grateful to have been a part of it."

Sophie managed a brief smile. "It meant a lot to both of us to have you and your family here. It was like having a piece of Concetta."

"Where will you go now?" Connie asked.

"Oh, don't worry about me. I'm far from broke. With the money I have from the sale of the house, I was able to buy a condo in Naples near my brother and his wife, and what's left will be a nice little nest egg. The condo is not as nice as what Damian and I would have bought if he were still alive, since he likely would have eventually drawn a salary again or gotten another job, but I'm turning over a new leaf to live more modestly. The death of a loved one puts things in perspective. All I really need is to be near family and to have a roof over my head."

When Connie had pulled up to Sophie's home and saw her sorrow, it was clear that Sophie was grieving for Damian. And Sophie couldn't have been leaning on her acting skills to make it appear that way, since she didn't know Connie was observing her. Sophie didn't stand to gain anything from Damian's death, so Connie mentally crossed Sophie off her list of suspects.

Maybe the police did have the right guy behind bars.

Connie placed her hand over Sophie's. "The reason I stopped by was to invite you to Christmas dinner on Wednesday at my house. I inherited the condo from Aunt Concetta after she passed away, so in a way, it would be like coming to her home." Now that Connie no longer suspected Sophie, it seemed like the right thing to do.

Sophie smiled warmly. "I appreciate the offer, but I'm having Christmas dinner with my brother and his family in Naples."

"Well, at least you can rest assured that the killer is behind bars," Connie said.

"I hope you're right."

Connie looked at Sophie with a questioning glance. "You mean you have your doubts that Rick is guilty?"

"At first, I thought he was, since he wanted Damian's position so badly. But the more I think about it, the less certain I am. I have known Rick for many years, and he and Damian have competed for many things, including the job of executive director. But Rick always played fair. I don't know how the cyanide ended up in his possession, but I have a hard time believing that he's a killer."

"It's definitely not Dottie," Connie said. "The police cleared her. I'm sure you heard that she was actually helping Damian."

"Yes, I know. I called her to apologize for the way I treated her. I even invited her over this morning and gave her some of Damian's memorabilia. She's a very kind woman. She's just lonely. Besides," she added, "anyone who thought so highly of my Damian can't be all that bad."

Connie was touched by Sophie's gesture.

"William was also on Damian's list of employees who would likely be laid off, but he had another job offer, so he doesn't have a motive," Connie said.

"I didn't realize that, and I don't blame him for jumping ship. He needs to earn a living."

"There aren't many people left. If you don't think Rick is the killer, is there someone else you suspect?"

Sophie lifted her palm towards Connie. "I'm done naming names. I going to trust in the justice system and let a jury decide about Rick. I learned my lesson from accusing Dottie."

Although Sophie didn't mention her by name, Connie couldn't help but notice the gigantic elephant in the room.

And the elephant's name was Eloise.

Chapter 19

AFTER HER CONVERSATION with Sophie, Connie returned to *Just Jewelry* to relieve Grace. It was difficult to keep busy, since it was a slow night, and all evening Sophie's words kept creeping into her mind. "I'm going to trust in the justice system and let a jury decide about Rick."

That was what Connie should do, too. Rick would have his day in court, and if he was innocent, the truth would prevail.

But she simply couldn't push from her mind the fact that Sophie, like Grace, who had known Rick for many years, didn't believe that he would hurt anyone.

Was Sophie right, or did Rick just snap?

Connie kept her thoughts about Rick's arrest to herself when she returned home later that evening, especially since Greg and Gary were still up, and she couldn't talk to her mother and sister alone. Everyone was so happy that the police had made an arrest, that Connie didn't want to ruin the moment for them with her skepticism. Besides, she could very well be wrong.

By Tuesday morning, although Connie still had her doubts, she had managed to put the whole situation out of her mind and keep her thoughts focused on Christmas Eve. Even though it wouldn't be a merry Christmas for Rick and Priscilla.

Connie had planned to keep the store open until noon on Christmas Eve, but by 11:00, she hadn't had a single customer. Just as she was contemplating closing the store early, Ruby scurried past her front door.

Connie opened the door and called out to Ruby, "Are you closing already?"

"I'm calling it a day," Ruby replied. "I haven't had a single customer all day, and there's no point sitting in there looking pretty. Many of the shops didn't even open today."

"See you on Thursday, then. Have a Merry Christmas."

Connie decided to follow Ruby's lead and close the store early.

With some extra time on her hands, now was as good a time as any to stop by the Sapphire Beach Playhouse to pick up Concetta's scrapbooks. The Christmas Eve performance was at noon, so if she left right away, she would have time to stop in before the play began. Fortunately, Jo and Gianna were preparing dinner, so once again, Connie didn't have to worry about cooking.

Since Connie still had Concetta's key to the administrative offices, she let herself into the boardroom to get the scrapbooks, then loaded them into the backseat of her car. While she was at the theatre, she decided to stop in to wish everyone a Merry Christmas.

The first people Connie ran into when she entered the lobby were Dottie and Maxine. Dottie was all smiles, clearly happy to be back as an usher.

"Hi ladies," Connie said. "Merry Christmas."

"Merry Christmas," the women said in unison.

As they were chatting about their Christmas plans, Eloise came into the lobby and joined them.

"I just dropped Stevie off backstage, and thought I'd stretch my legs. Besides," she added with a wink, "he already doesn't like his mom constantly hanging around him, and he's not even a teenager yet."

"Oh boy, it's starting already," Connie joked.

"I'm so glad you decided to come back to the theatre, Dottie," Eloise said. "It would have been a shame to let a threatening note keep you away from what you love doing."

"She's one resilient woman," Connie said with an encouraging smile.

Maxine excused herself and went back to her station.

After they chatted for a few minutes, Eloise had to check on her son. "Excuse me while I go keep an eye on Stevie while pretending to do something else," she said with a slight roll of her eyes.

"I have to go, as well," Connie said. "I want to wish some members of the cast a Merry Christmas while I'm here."

Connie started down the main aisle in the theatre toward the stage when it suddenly occurred to her.

While everyone knew that Dottie had disappeared, she hadn't told anyone besides Connie and Zach that she received a threatening note. The only way Eloise could have known about it was if she wrote it herself.

Connie's heart was beating rapidly in her chest. She turned around to look at Dottie, who stood facing her at the end of the aisle. Judging from the look of terror on Dottie's face, she pieced it together the same time as Connie.

Connie picked up her pace and made a beeline backstage. She approached Eloise, who stood by the side entrance to the stage.

"Eloise, how did you know that Dottie received a threatening note?"

Her eyes flew wide open. "I...I don't know. Dottie must have told me."

"Did you kill Damian and send Dottie that note to keep her quiet about what she overheard?"

"Of course not. Please, keep your voice down, Connie. I told you, Dottie must have mentioned the note to me."

"Okay, then, I'll go ask her." Connie started back toward the lobby.

"Wait."

She turned to face Eloise. "I'm listening."

Eloise glanced around, apparently to be sure nobody could overhear. There was a flurry of activity around them, and the actors were busy getting into character and performing vocal exercises, since the show would be starting shortly. Eloise straightened her shoulders and looked directly at Connie. "I did slip Dottie the note. But I swear, I would never have hurt Damian. I only wanted to keep her quiet about the conversation she overheard between Damian and me. It was extremely personal, and if she repeated any of it, it could have destroyed my family. I realize in hindsight that I shouldn't have threatened her. I was so scared that I wasn't thinking straight. It didn't occur to me until she left town how she might have interpreted it."

Eloise's explanation did make sense. If Dottie had repeated what she overheard, it would have cost Eloise dearly. While sending Dottie the note was a gross misjudgment, it didn't necessarily make her a killer.

If Eloise wasn't the killer, Connie was officially out of suspects. Rick was looking more and more guilty.

"I guess I can believe that it could have been a misunderstanding," Connie said. "It's just so hard to believe that Rick is a killer."

"I know," Eloise said. "I'm struggling with that, too."

"I guess bankruptcy is the least of his problems now."

"What do you mean by bankruptcy? Why would Rick declare bankruptcy?"

"William told me that Rick was heavily in debt and needed his job with the playhouse to avoid financial ruin."

Eloise stroked her chin. "That doesn't make any sense. When Rick learned that Damian was no longer drawing a salary from the playhouse, he agreed to stop taking one, too. He said he recently received a substantial inheritance from his parents, and it was enough so that he didn't have to worry about money."

"Then why would William have told me that?" Connie asked. "William said that he didn't want to find himself in Rick's position, so that was why he is moving to Sarasota - to take a job with a playhouse there."

"What are you talking about?" Eloise asked. "My best friend is the executive director for that playhouse. I would know if there were any positions open there."

"Are you sure, Eloise?"

"Positive. She is forever trying to convince me to work for her. Every time there is an opening in the artistic department, she calls me in hopes that I'll consider taking the job. There haven't been any openings this entire year."

"If William never planned to leave the Sapphire Beach Playhouse, then he had every reason to want Damian out of the picture," Connie said, slowly piecing together the puzzle.

Eloise's jaw dropped as she motioned for Connie to look behind her. Connie slowly turned around to meet the penetrating gaze of an angry Scrooge glaring at her from behind one of the red velvet curtain panels.

"William," Connie said. "I can't believe I didn't see it before. You killed Damian to save your job."

"You're crazy! I did no such thing."

"Damian was going lay you off, and you had nothing to fall back on," Connie said. "You made up that job offer in Sarasota."

A vein bulged from William's forehead. "I'm better than any actor in that theatre. There just weren't any openings." He clenched his fists. "Damian got what was coming to him. It wasn't enough for him to run the playhouse into the ground. He had to take the lead role in what might be our last Christmas production. When I told Damian that I wanted to play Scrooge this year, he just laughed at me. Who's getting the last laugh now?" William pointed an index finger at Connie and Eloise. "You two can't prove a thing."

"We're going to the police right now," Connie said. She grabbed Eloise's hand, and the two women stepped around William to make a quick exit. William turned to lunge at them, but he froze before his foot even left the ground. All three of them stood motionless as they watched the front curtain rise. William had no choice but to walk onstage for what Connie could only guess would be the last performance of his career.

"I'm going to call the police," Connie said to Eloise once William was a safe distance away.

A voice came from behind her. "I already did. They'll be here shortly."

It was Dottie.

"I saw you disappear backstage with her," she said, pointing to Eloise. "When you didn't come back, I decided to play it safe."

"The killer is William, not Eloise," Connie said to Dottie.

"But I can understand why you thought I was dangerous," Eloise said. "Can you ever forgive me for sending you that note?"

"I guess I can understand why you were afraid," Dottie said. "I may be a little too fanatical when it comes to my favorite actors, but I'm not a gossip."

Dottie returned to the lobby to meet the police and escort them to Connie and Eloise.

It felt like a strange dream as Connie watched the first half of the show hoping the police would arrive before the intermission. She breathed a deep sigh of relief when Dottie and Zach arrived backstage with only a few minutes to spare. Then Dottie returned to her station to tend to her intermission responsibilities.

When William exited the stage and found Zach standing with Connie and Eloise, he shook his head. "Detective, these women are nothing but busybodies. I'm sorry they wasted your time."

Members of the cast and crew were scurrying about all around them.

"Is there a place we can talk in private?" Zach asked.

Judith, who had been watching the production from the other side of the stage, made her way over when she saw Zach arrive and insisted on joining them.

William led them to his dressing room - the same room where Damian was killed.

Connie and Eloise explained everything they had discovered, as well as their earlier conversation with William when he admitted to killing Damian.

"These women are crazy," William said to Zach. Then he looked at Judith. "Honey, they can't prove any of this."

Judith began to tremble, and tears streamed down her cheeks. When she finally composed herself, she made eye contact with each person in the room. "They can't prove it, but I can. William, the cyanide in the garage? The antacid you purchased before the play? And the lies. You asked me to tell the police that you were with me when Damian was poisoned. I convinced myself that it was okay, because there was no way my husband could do such a thing. But..." she sobbed. "Why, William? Why did you switch the bottle of antacid that Rick had bought? Wasn't it enough to kill Damian? Did you have to frame Rick, too?"

"I did it for us. For our future. We were never so happy as we have been in Sapphire Beach, and Damian was going to take that away from us. And without Rick, I'd have had seniority."

There was a knock on the dressing room door. "Five minutes 'til curtain, William."

"Thanks, five," William replied somberly. He looked at Zach with pleading eyes. "Can I finish my performance?"

Zach was silent for what seemed like an eternity.

"Can't you let him finish for the sake of the playhouse?" Connie asked. "It would be a shame to cut short the Christmas Eve performance."

"Okay," Zach said. "But I'll be waiting for you when you finish."

Zach accompanied William back to the stage while Connie followed a short distance behind. Eloise stayed with Judith to comfort her.

As Connie watched William give the performance of a lifetime, she couldn't help but be struck by the irony. He was pouring out his heart in the role of Scrooge, a character who learned that greed and selfishness don't pay off in the end. Yet what greedier and more selfish act could there be than taking the life of another?

Chapter 20

EARLY CHRISTMAS MORNING, Connie awoke to the sound of two three-year-olds in Rudolph-the-Red-Nosed Reindeer pajamas tugging on her arm and a tired Gianna smiling in the doorway. "They blocked their eyes as they walked through the living room to get to your bedroom, but there's no more holding back this tidal wave," she said laughing.

With a shot of Christmas-fueled adrenaline, Connie jumped out of bed and scooped the twins into her arms. "Let's go see what Santa brought you two little monkeys," she said, carrying them to the living room where Gary, her parents, and Grace had already assembled.

The children's excitement turned into awe as they took in the scene before them.

"Look," Gary said, holding up a plate of crumbs and carrot stubs. "It looks like Santa and the reindeer ate the treats we left for them last night."

Hannah and Noah stared wide-eyed at the crumbs. Then they scanned the toys under the tree, and with expressions of amazement, looked at their parents.

"Look at the toys Santa brought you. You must have been good children this year," Gianna said, while Gary recorded the scene with his phone.

As Connie watched her niece and nephew explore the gifts under the tree, the previous day's events at the playhouse seemed like a distant memory. The morning flew by, and by the time Gary and Greg assembled a few toys for the twins to play with and everyone showered and got ready, it was nearly time for company to arrive.

Connie and Gianna went to work preparing appetizers, while Jo made the lasagna. Once the stuffed mushrooms, spinach pastries, and tomatoes with basil and mozzarella cheese were heating in the oven, they sat by the tree to wait for their guests.

The Millers were the first to arrive with Gertrude. Emma proudly carried a pink frosted cake that she made herself. "Can I tell them now, Mom?" Emma asked, unable to contain her excitement.

Elyse smiled broadly. "Go ahead, honey."

"I made this cake so we could celebrate that Victoria is now officially my little sister."

Elyse and Josh beamed with pride as Emma announced the news.

"It's the best Christmas present we could have received," Elyse said, slipping her arms around Josh's waist.

"That is so kind of you to share your celebration with us," Jo said as she placed the cake on a counter with the wine and other desserts. "I can't wait to taste it."

Stephanie arrived next, followed by Zach.

Within no time, Connie's home was bustling with Christmas activity. Gary selected a Christmas playlist, and everyone gathered in the living room to enjoy a glass of wine and some appetizers while the children played and the lasagna finished baking. The lights on the Christmas tree they had decorated together reflected off the gold garland and provided a festive ambiance. Even Ginger seemed to be enjoying the day, as she relaxed in the sun by the sliders and chewed on a rawhide bone she received in her stocking.

Jo smiled warmly at Ginger, but then her gaze turned more serious as it settled on the crystal blue waters beyond the double slider.

"A penny for your thoughts," Greg said to his wife.

"I still can't believe that Judith had to turn in her own husband," Jo said.

"Yes, she was in a no-win situation." Greg cast a mischievous grin Connie's way, then looked back at his wife. "Let me ask you... if *your* husband was guilty of a crime, say breaking and entering at night, for example, would you turn him in?"

Connie couldn't help but laugh as she remembered hiding out with her father in the boardroom at the administrative offices of the Sapphire Beach Playhouse.

Jo winked at her husband. "Never."

Josh shot Zach an amused glance. "I don't even want to know," he said.

"When I first met Judith in my shop a couple of weeks ago, she appeared to be shallow and gossipy,"

Connie said. "But you have to admire her for doing the right thing when it counted."

"I never did thank you for taking care of everything last night so I could spend Christmas Eve with my family," Josh said to Zach. "What time did you get home?"

"I don't remember, but it was late," Zach said. "I didn't want Rick to have to spend Christmas in jail, so I wanted to take care of things before leaving for the holiday. Rick was a free man by the time I got home."

"That reminds me," Connie said. "Sophie called this morning while I was waiting for the shower. She wanted us to know how grateful she was that the right person is in jail for her husband's murder. She also said that she stopped by Rick's and Priscilla's house on her way to her brother's this morning to wish them a Merry Christmas and tell them how sorry she was for everything they had been through. The three of them got to talking about the future of the Sapphire Beach Playhouse, and Sophie is going to recommend Rick as the new permanent executive director. She said that both Rick and Priscilla had some fantastic fundraising ideas so she and Priscilla are going to work as Rick's assistants, free of charge, so they can quickly implement Rick's ideas, and some of Damian's that he never had the chance to try. In light of everything that happened, she said the staff is really banding together as a family. She is confident that the Board of Directors will agree to their plan."

"I'm happy that we are finally seeing something positive come out this tragedy," Greg said. "If they work with one another, rather than against each other, they might just get the job done."

"I have one more announcement," Connie said. "I received an email yesterday from Dura saying that the parish will begin construction on the chicken coop right after the first of the year. The local families said it was an answer to their Christmas prayers."

"That's fantastic," Gianna said.

"And that's not all. Since Damian purchased so many pairs of earrings, Dura and her pastor agreed to name the project in his memory. They're calling it The Damian Pritchard Chicken Coop."

"That's a beautiful way to honor his memory," Zach said.

"His generosity means even more, since it came at a time when he and Sophie were struggling financially," Connie said.

"Speaking of candy cane earrings, did you ever figure out who the earring belonged to that was found near Damian's body?" Gianna asked Zach. "It clearly wasn't William's."

"Yes, we figured that out early on. It belonged to Sophie. She thinks she lost it when she discovered her husband's body and fell to her knees. But with the shock of losing her husband, she didn't even realize it was missing until we asked her about it later that night."

"And what about Stevie?" Jo asked. "Did Sophie or Stephen ever find out that Stevie is Damian's son?"

"We never told them," Zach said. "There was no reason to."

"I think that was a wise decision," Jo said. "Stevie seems like a happy little boy. Why ruin that?"

"Exactly," Zach said. "It should be Eloise's decision when and how much to tell them."

The oven timer sounded, indicating that Christmas dinner was ready, so the group moved to the dining room table. Connie, Gianna, Elyse, and Stephanie made quick work of slicing and serving the lasagna and putting the meatballs, sausages, and salad on the table.

After Greg prayed the blessing, Jo said, "Let's not talk about murder over Christmas dinner."

Connie wholeheartedly agreed. Christmas was a day to be contemplating the joy and wonder of the season, not the selfish and greedy act of one man. As Connie looked around the table at so many of the people she loved and cared for, she wished this meal could last forever. The only thing missing was the company of those no longer with them.

Connie felt Zach's warm gaze and turned to face him. He smiled and took her hand beneath the table, as if he had been reading her thoughts. He leaned closer and whispered, "It's like we were saying on our date: perfect joy is only for heaven."

Connie squeezed his hand. "Yes, but this is pretty close."

Next Book in this Series

Book 5: *Snowbirds and Suspects*
Available on Amazon

OR

Free Prequel: *Vacations and Victims*
Meet Concetta and Bethany in the
Sapphire Beach prequel.
Available in ebook or PDF format only at:
BookHip.com/MWHDFP

Stay in touch!

Join my Readers' Group for periodic updates, exclusive content, and to be notified of new releases. Enter your email address at:
BookHip.com/MWHDFP

OR

Email:
angela@angelakryan.com

Facebook:
facebook.com/AngelaKRyanAuthor

Post Office:
Angela K. Ryan, John Paul Publishing, P.O. Box 283, Tewksbury, MA 01876

ABOUT THE AUTHOR

Angela K. Ryan, author of the *Sapphire Beach Cozy Mystery Series*, writes clean, feel-good stories that uplift and inspire, with mysteries that will keep you guessing.

When she is not writing, Angela enjoys the outdoors, especially kayaking, stand-up paddleboarding, snowshoeing, and skiing. She lives near Boston and loves the change of seasons in New England, but, like her main character, she looks forward to brief escapes to the white, sandy beaches of southwest Florida, where her mother resides.

Angela dreams of one day owning a Cavalier King Charles Spaniel like Ginger, but isn't home enough to take care of one. So, for now, she lives vicariously through her main character, Connie.

Made in United States
North Haven, CT
12 January 2022

14665456R00150